BETWEEN THE BOUNDARIES

ESSAYS

Adam Somerset is a writer and critic. His work on Welsh theatre has become an ongoing conversation with culture and society that has extended to art, photography, television and radio, history and politics. After earlier careers in industry he has lived in Ceredigion since 1991. His work has appeared extensively in journals, newspapers and on-line.

BETWEEN THE BOUNDARIES

ESSAYS

ADAM SOMERSET

PARTHIAN

Parthian, Cardigan SA43 1ED
www.parthianbooks.com
First published in 2019
© Adam Somerset 2019
ISBN 978-1-912681-36-5
Editor: Carly Holmes
Cover design: Eddie Matthews
Cover image: Adam Somerset, from a pastel drawing by Sue Cottrell
Typeset by Elaine Sharples
Printed by 4edge Limited
Published with the financial support of the Welsh Books Council.
British Library Cataloguing in Publication Data
A cataloguing record for this book is available from the British Library.

CONTENTS

Introduction   1

Art and the Anthropocene   5

Arab Spring to Winter in 155 Steps   14

Doctor Dee and the Exemplar Number of All Things
Numerable   21

A Liberal Retrospective   26

We Became Orphans: A Writer in the Yucatan   35

A Visit to the Cloud   45

Wherever There Is Arbitrariness, There Is Also a Certain
Regularity   51

War: What Is it Good For?   57

The Digital Superhighway   62

Waiting for a Beaver   67

I'll Swap You Two Buggers for a Shit   72

An Elephant in Bremen   81

The Hate Horrifies Me   87

Who Needs Empathy? Automating the Professionals   95

I Long the Arrival of the Ship with the Seeds   102

An Occasional Flash of Silliness   112

The Map-makers   118

A Citizen's Guide to the European Union   125

They Are Obsessed by Fear   130

Among the Demonstrators   138

Arnold Potts   146

Clarice Beckett   153

Our Water Closet Has Been Stopt   159

A Small Blip for Big Gig   166

A Pint, a Poet and a Portrait   172

Brits Don't Quit   177

Acknowledgements   184

Bibliography   185

Index of Places   191

Index of People   197

Introduction
Essays in History, Art & Work

Between the Boundaries comprises twenty-six essays on subjects that came my way over the course of a year. The subjects divide in two. Seventeen are of public events – literary, political, artistic – and nine are a result of visits in Wales, England, Germany and Australia. The triggers varied. On two occasions organisers sent me invitations to attend. Three came about as a result of being in the company of friends. But the majority were wholly serendipitous. An impromptu stop on a journey revealed something unexpected and interesting. A poster, a brochure or a website indicated an event that was out of the ordinary.

2016 was a pivotal year for the politics of the United Kingdom. "A caesura in our national history and our place in the world, a guillotine moment", is how Peter Hennessy, the political historian, puts it in 'Among the Demonstrators'. Europe is the subject of the commemorative lecture in 'A Liberal Retrospective'. Mid-year a Cambridge political scientist delivered, in print and on a public platform, his 'A Citizen's Guide to the European Union'. The last essay, 'Brits Don't Quit', connects the Shadow Foreign Secretary, as he then was, to the art of William Hogarth. A European author is the subject of 'I Long the Arrival of the Ship with the Seeds'. On her first arrival in Britain she was startled by the differences from home. "Europe versus Britain", runs the final line, "so close, so different."

The visual arts are the subject of six essays. In 'A Pint, a Poet and a Portrait' three artists depict Dylan Thomas. A good proportion of the paintings of 'Clarice Beckett' suffered an unusual fate in being eaten by insects. Hers was an art of close-up observation of a world no more than a mile or so from her home. By contrast, in 'Art and the Anthropocene' artists grapple with the challenge of representing a planet in change over millennia. In 'The Map-makers' artists are employed in clandestine wartime service. A public monument, the sculpture in 'An Elephant in Bremen', is given a new meaning that is the exact opposite to the one at the time of its unveiling sixty years previously. In 'The Digital Superhighway' art and technology intersect uneasily.

Technology features in other essays. 'I'll Swap You Two Buggers for a Shit' is a tale from another age. One and a half million pounds worth of computers sits unopened in its packing. Management is unable to enforce their usage. 'A Visit to the Cloud' is the opposite to the suggestion of its title, its location being an underground bunker protected within layers of steel and concrete. 'Who Needs Empathy?' suggests that quite a lot of us do, and that the rule of the robots may not be quite so dominant as the most extreme doom-sayers predict. The judicial minds in 'A Small Blip for Big Gig' give Big Tech their firm thumbs-down. Their reasoning is as much driven by the company's weird stretching of common language as for its innovatory business practices. In 'Wherever There Is Arbitrariness, There Is Also a Certain Regularity' a mathematician travels to Poland in 1938 and is informed it is a key principle for decryption.

As for the title of the book, the subjects may have been serendipitous. But, as Dennis Potter once phrased it, the contours of a life are marked out by a few obsessions. The word "border" occurs regularly. There are genuine borders here. The Roman camp at Vindolanda in 'War: What Is it Good For?' was a line between Empire and beyond. Allied prisoners of war in Germany received maps of silk under board games that had been ostensibly gifted by charities. These maps showed the border with Switzerland and the best routes for escape. By contrast, the citizens of the German Democratic Republic placed themselves in hazard when they attempted to cross the borders of Bulgaria or Hungary. Their government had fabricated maps in which borders were falsified.

Borders are crossable. As described in 'They Are Obsessed by Fear' diamonds in the present day cross borders embedded in tubes of toothpaste. Borders, underpinned by law and by arms, are argued over and amendable. Boundaries are slacker and looser but as ubiquitous, potent and disputable. Geological definitions require a specific boundary between layers of rock. The concept of the era of the Holocene was established by the difference between two ice layers extracted from a core from Greenland. In 'They Are Obsessed by Fear' the economist points to the paradox of tax. Jurisdictions are confined within borders where economic organisations are not.

Lord Berners in 'An Occasional Flash of Silliness' plays with the boundaries of convention in the way his friend Dali upended time and space in his painting. Boundaries that are conventional are held up for question. Art and science are commonly presented as antagonists. Sir Humphrey Davy is just one to see "the truths of the natural sciences" as "analogy to the productions of the refined arts". As for the ultimate barrier – that between the here and now, the world of time and space, and another realm – in 'Doctor Dee and the Exemplar Number of All Things Numerable', the transcendent is there for the grasping.

The tradition of John Dee belongs to a minority. George Orwell in 'Among the Demonstrators' is cited on his compatriots: "They have a horror of abstract thought, they feel no need for any philosophy or systematic 'worldview'". Dee and Orwell are the polar points of idealism versus pragmatism. Europe, as in 'A Citizen's Guide to the European Union', was never just an arrangement of economic instrumentalism. Descartes, Fichte and Locke are the ghosts who hover and are little spoken of. Virtual boundary lines are powerful semantic markers. Their influence is as strong as the lines which delineate physical territory; hence the title for these essays that walk between the boundaries.

Art and the Anthropocene

Shakespeare knew every word in the English language. That gave him knowledge of every activity undertaken by his compatriots. There was no human action that was not available for him to use as illustration or metaphor. The number of words in the language has since grown thirty-fold. Shakespeare knew the world of humans in its entirety. The world now is known only by the gigantic human hive-mind, far beyond the grasp of any single consciousness.

Applications for jobs employ words that are not comprehensible by the layperson. The language is itself a sifting mechanism for pre-selection. Dictionaries race after neologisms and churn archaisms. Legions of words are lost, within a generation, from common knowledge or are limited in geography. A toot in the west of England is an isolated hill ideally suited to be a look-out. An aquabob in Kent is an icicle. A bleb in the north is a bubble of air contained within ice.

The *Dictionary of American Regional English* contains many words unknown on the Atlantic's eastern shore. To "pungle up" means to produce money that is owed. "The mulligrubs" mean indigestion and, by extension, a bad mood overall. Many of these terms never made it to print. For those that did, the scanning of books from past centuries opens them up to analysis. The rate of word extinction is speeding up. Some, like "frog strangler" for heavy rain, have made way for plain "downpour". Some have proved redundant. "Radiogram" and "Roentgenogram" have given way to "X-ray", which is the same process. Sometimes it seems they are not wanted. "Respair" in the sense of a return of hope after a period of despair sounds useful. But the last record of its use was in 1425.

The words that have receded are those of Saxon origin and the new are Latin or Greek in their origins. In writing a book review Anthony Burgess came up against a linguistic gap. With no word for the making of a stamp he invented "intimbration". Boris Johnson, a classicist, makes free use of "eirenic" and "ataraxic". The first indicates peace-seeking, the second serene indifference. A recent review of a poetry collection by R S Thomas used the word "stratiographic". The Anthropocene is a staple of the sciences that has spread to take root in literary criticism. Until this gathering of scientists and artists in Aberystwyth the word had been unknown to me.

The notion of geological timescales was conceived by the British geologist Arthur Holmes in 1913. The discovery of radio-activity led to the Earth being aged at around 4.5 billion years. Geology moves in large intervals of time. An aeon is its longest period of time with four to date, lasting half a billion years or more. Then come eras, ten of several hundred million years, and periods, twenty-two of them of one hundred million years. Epochs are measured in tens of millions of years and ages in mere millions. The present geological era, the Holocene, has lasted twelve thousand years.

An Anthropocene Working Group of the Subcommission on Quaternary Stratigraphy was created in 2009. It had two areas for deliberation: whether the Anthropocene should be formalised as an epoch, and, if so, to determine when it began. The suggested start-points are various. It could equally be the first recorded use of fire by hominids, 1.8m years ago, the beginning of agriculture, eight thousand years ago, or the Industrial Revolution. Geological change is possessed of an inexorable slowness. The scientists charged with its classification are not inclined to peremptory decision-making.

The concept that humanity itself has become the leading determinant of the earth's physical fabric goes back to the last century. A conference was held in Mexico City in 1999 on the Holocene, the epoch that began around 11,700 years ago. The Nobel prize-winning atmospheric chemist Paul Crutzen wavered against consensus. "I suddenly thought this was wrong" was his later recollection. "The world has changed too much. So I said, 'No, we are in the Anthropocene.' I just made the word up on the spur of the moment. But it seems to have stuck."

Crutzen, in collaboration with Eugene Stoermer, published the following year an article that proposed that the Anthropocene be considered a new epoch for the Earth. Its central thesis was that "mankind will remain a major geological force for many millennia, maybe millions of years to come". The eminence of the authors was such that the Crutzen-Stoermer proposition was considered with seriousness. It was time for the stratigraphers to enter. Stratigraphers have been called the archivists, the monks, the philosophers even, of the Earth sciences. They look to the workings of deep time and its division. They move in aeons and epochs; their task is the classification in time of division and subdivision. Their guide, and authority, is the International Chronostratigraphic Chart that archives our Earth from now back to the era of the Hadean, 4bn to 4.6bn years ago.

The evidence for declaring this the age of the Anthropocene is manifest. The future limestones of the Earth will be made from creatures whose shells are being altered by acidic changes in the sea. In 1750 about 5% of the planet's surface was farmed, a percentage that has grown to 50%. That has required nitrogen and dams. Silt by the billions of tonnes has ceased to move much distance. Everywhere river deltas are shrinking. The doubling of nitrogen and phosphorous in soils in the past century makes the largest impact on the nitrogen cycle in 2.5bn years. A new concept of technofossils has emerged. New types of minerals may emerge from the deposition of elemental aluminium in soil. It has no existence in untransformed nature. The fly ash from power stations may consolidate into novel rocks. Plutonium is rare in nature but is now scattered across the planet after the testing of nuclear weaponry. The geologists of times to come will see a layer of plutonium or uranium within rock.

The numbers behind humanity's urge to make are awesome. Since 1945, the volume of concrete, aluminium and plastic manufactured is collectively the greatest mineral change in 2.4bn years. Fifty billion metric tonnes of concrete have been produced, half in the last twenty years. But geological division is not a matter of dates. It requires a specific boundary between layers of rock. In the case of the Holocene the boundary was between two ice layers in a core taken from Greenland.

Scientists are thus at work on sites where annual layers are formed. They are at the mud sediments that form off the coast of Santa Barbara in California and in the Ernesto cave in Italy, whose stalactites and stalagmites accrue annual rings. Lake sediments, ice cores, corals, tree rings, layers of rubbish in landfill even, are all being investigated. Results are not expected to be sudden. "If we were very lucky and someone came forward with, say, a core from a classic example of laminated sediments in a deep marine environment, I think three years is possibly viable," says a researcher. But, he says, "Our stratigraphic colleagues are very protective of the geological time scale. They see it very rightly as the backbone of geology and they do not amend it lightly." The decision to officially designate the age of the Anthropocene will be a vote at a meeting of the International Union of Geological Sciences.

The age of the Anthropocene is played out on the grandest of scales. Humans have made forty-eight thousand large dams. These dams, in combination with ground water extraction, are the cause of shrinking deltas. Annual consumption of coal is 4.5 million metric tonnes, and forecast to rise to 6.9 million by 2030. Rivers in aggregate still shift sediment by the billions of tonnes. Humans create thirteen billion tonnes of aggregate and mine eight billion tonnes of coal. Soil loss is cited as seventy-five billion tonnes. A sixth great extinction is in prospect as a result of a mix of encroachment on habitats, pollution, disease and introduced species.

* * * *

These numbers are vast and alarming. To be eighty kilograms of organo-chemical substance with a life-span of eight decades feels small indeed. But then the great intervals of geological time are outstripped by bigger numbers. A single human brain may sputter out after its short time but two and a half kilograms of skull-enclosed mushy substance does its work via big numbers. Synapses and signals are measured in the trillions. On this day those trillions are amplified by a gathering of carbon-based bipeds. Aberystwyth's Arts Centre has attracted a diverse and good collection for a day that is titled *Strata: art and science collaborations in the Anthropocene*.

The organisations behind the day event cover an unusual span. Acknowledgements are given to the Arts Centre, the University's School of Art and the Department of Geography and Earth Sciences. From further away the Visualising Geomorphology Working Group of the British Society for Geomorphology is a supporting participant. This is not the first time that this cluster across the sciences and arts have combined. This group has form.

Previous conference-exhibition-installations have roamed the border territory of the domains of science and art. Jony Easterby is an artist, but an artist of landscape. His media are not brush and watercolour but the real-world material of nature. He is an agent of transformation who comes to an upland plot high above the River Dyfi. Rugged highland is transformed into a seeded, more productive, more bio-diverse alternative. And it is also more aesthetic. Anthony Burgess in the course of writing on Hemingway made a throwaway comment that artists need to know about more than art. They need to know about things. Jony Easterby may be an artist but he knows the earth that he remakes. He knows soils and clays, the acids and the alkalis that inhibit the flourishing of plant life.

He is the representative of artist and earth. Jane Lloyd Francis' attention is to water. The rivers of Wales are well documented. The great artificial enclosures of water, the reservoirs for cities elsewhere, are the possession of investment banks and hedge funds. Jane Lloyd Francis is in pursuit of those sources of water that are older, smaller, more elusive, often hidden. Her subject is the tiny wells that watered the fledgling communities of inland Wales. In near-lost places, essential to both individual and community life, they took on meanings of symbol and holiness. The well that succoured nearby Taliesin is now a culvert beneath an A-road. The ancient well of Machynlleth is now within a residential home whose architectural parts span centuries.

This combination, geographers and artists, had created another previous event on the theme *Future Climate Dialogues*. On that occasion Mark Macklin, a Professor of Physical Geography, displayed photographs of river basins that were the study of a fluvial geomorphologist. They were placed side by side with abstractly patterned lino-prints. The forms from nature and the artistic imagination are mirrors to each other. The geomorphologist explained the origin of his research. Its fuel is recognition of pattern, conceptualisation, the capacity to envisage a site three-dimensionally. He is in the tradition of predecessor scientists. August Kekulé grasped the structure of the benzene ring while daydreaming on a bus. Leo Szilard conceived the notion of a nuclear chain reaction from the switch of colour on a Bloomsbury Square traffic light.

* * * *

Art of greatness has performed a later unexpected function as a window for science. Doctors have gazed into the canvases of Hans

Memling and recognised the piercing sharpness of the artist's fifteenth-century eye. Memling depicted pathologies that were to wait five hundred years for diagnosis and classification. Glaciolologist Mike Hambrey in Aberystwyth displays the landscape paintings made by Thomas Fearnley. The artist died in 1842 but his paintings of the Grindelwald and other glaciers are minutely accurate in their detail and colouring. They are eloquent pointers to the effects of climate change.

Science enriches artistic appreciation. John Gerald's *Herball* of 1597 is a guide to a pre-herbicidal British field threaded with the toxins of choke, earcockle, endophyte and ergot. The Little Ice Age, the series of disastrous harvests that led to the food riots of 1607, is manifestly there in the work of Shakespeare. He was its witness.

The introduction for today revisits the putative gap between the two domains of science and art. That they are distinct is true; that they are a dichotomy is not so. For every Blake with his "Art is the tree of life. Science is the tree of death", there is a rebuttal. Sir Humphrey Davy is as great an exponent of science as any. He saw in "the truths of the natural sciences ... analogy to the productions of the refined arts. The contemplation of the laws of the universe is connected with an immediate tranquil exaltation of mind, and pure mental enjoyment. The perception of truth is almost as simple a feeling as the perception of beauty; and the genius of Newton, of Shakespeare, of Michaelangelo, and of Händel, are not very remote in character from each other."

Davy in the nineteenth century prefigures the working method of Mark Macklin in the twenty-first. "Imagination, as well as the reason, is necessary to perfection in the philosophic mind", wrote Davy. "A rapidity of combination, a power of perceiving analogies, and comparing them by facts, is the creative source of discovery. Discrimination and delicacy of sensation, so important in physical research, are other words for taste; and the love of nature is the same passion as the love of the magnificent, the sublime, and the beautiful."

If science must be gradual in its deliberations, art has no brake. The artists who have come to Aberystwyth have made their work in the Bristol Channel, on the Medway estuary, in Alaska. Their works are small in scale and still exploratory, but in Munich the Deutsches Museum is a very large institution. It has mounted *An Anthropocene Wunderkammer*, a Chamber of Wonders. The American writer and conservation biologist Julianne Lutz Warren has a work there. *Hopes Echo* remembers the huia, an exquisite bird of New Zealand. It became extinct a century ago due to habitat destruction, the arrival of predators and the lure to hunters of its black and ivory tail feathers. It was rendered extinct before its song was recorded.

But its song was mimicked by people and this mimicked song was passed down across the generations. In 1954 a New Zealander, R A L Batley, made a recording of a Maori man, Henare Hamana, whistling his imitation of the huia's call. This recording is the sonic substrate for Warren's exhibit. "It is", she says, "a soundtrack of the sacred voices of extinct birds echoing in that of a dead man echoing out of a machine echoing through the world today."

The art of the Anthropocene has its core themes of loss and vanishing. In the sixth great extinction a third of amphibian species is at risk and a fifth of five and a half thousand known mammals are classified as endangered, threatened or vulnerable. The scale is so great that individual art works seem too miniscule in response. But words are universal signifiers outside time. A lexicography for the Anthropocene has launched itself. In 2014 *The Bureau of Linguistical Reality* was founded. Its function is "the purpose of collecting, translating and creating a new vocabulary for the Anthropocene". Solastalgia is there, along with "stieg", "apex-guilt" and "shadowtime". The last means "The sense of living in two or more orders of temporal scale simultaneously."

If there is a best word to summarise this Aberystwyth assembly it is "hyperobject". The word has been in existence for a time but Timothy Morton adopted it in 2010 to denote some of the characteristic entities of the Anthropocene. Hyperobjects are "so massively distributed in time, space and dimensionality" as to be outside our perception and largely beyond our comprehension. Morton's examples of hyperobjects are climate change, mass species extinction, radioactive plutonium. They are abstractions. Beyond perception they invite denial. But, says Morton, "they are ferociously, catastrophically real."

Our own timescale is a hyperobject. With a starting-point four and a half billion years ago a third rock from the sun spun itself from a clump of material into a coalescing planet. A rock of some size collided with it and knocked away the moon. It received a tilt that became the cause of seasons and currents. The knocked-off part makes the tides. After half a billion years conditions were right for life. For three and a half billion years the climate oscillated between extreme glaciations. Eventually the environment became right for multicellular life-forms of complexity.

Geology, chemistry and biology interacted and acted upon the rock. Roots exacerbated the breakdown of rigid physical structure. Channels caught rain water and led to rivers. Photosynthesis worked its wonders. In the great clock of time, close to midnight, a biped species emerged. It is not alone in making and using tools, nor in organising work by specialisation, but it is better at both than any other species. The universe has no intrinsic knowledge of itself. Its self-knowledge is wholly contained within the squeaks, the blurts and marks made by several billion pieces of short-dated organo-chemical material. The world's naming has long been the work of women and men and now it is of their making too.

The Anthropocene itself entered the *Oxford English Dictionary* late. It made its debut in June 2014, the same year as "selfie". As a juxtaposition it could not be nicer.

January 2016: Aberystwyth

Arab Spring to Winter in 155 Steps

Dr Alaa Al-Aswany is away from his home city of Cairo for promotion of his novel, *The Automobile Club of Egypt*. His earlier novel, *The Yacoubian Building*, is among the most translated of the century from an author whose writing language is not English. He is also a public intellectual, having been both participant in and witness to the Revolution of 2011. In the years that followed he wrote a lengthy weekly essay for newspaper publication. They numbered one hundred and fifty-five and have now ceased. But they are gathered in book form under the title *Democracy is the Answer*, the sentence with which he closed each piece. Al-Aswany is also a dentist and he threads his talk with episodes from his experience and on occasion with metaphors taken from medicine.

Arab Spring – Arab Winter is the title for an event that describes itself as a public discussion. The host organisation is the Ralph Miliband Programme within the London School of Economics. The talk is part of a sequence entitled *Progress and its Discontents*. The format is that Al-Aswany is invited to speak for twenty minutes before the floor is opened for questions. He is a figure in middle age, in formal suit and tie, weightier and darker in complexion than the press photographs suggest. He remains seated and comes without slide illustrations. His voice is low in tone and he is completely compelling.

His audience is young and the questioners are international. A curly-haired questioner of some youth describes himself simply as a post-graduate student. From his question it is clear that he too was in Egypt in 2011 at the heart of the Revolution. A voice from

14

the gallery identifies herself professionally as a charity worker. Al-Aswany has looked at, and drawn comparison with, other revolutions. The question about the comparison with the revolution of Romania has a particular pointedness in that the asker is herself a Romanian.

Many novelists take on a second activity of journalism but they are usually more than journalists. Al-Aswany displays a knowledge of history in its depth and geography in its breadth. But like all good public discourse his arguments rest on a basic simplicity. Democracy really is the answer. Inevitably a questioner is on hand to suggest that Islam itself may be antithetical to a democratic state. Al-Aswany has the facts from his country at his fingertips. He knows the voting patterns in historic elections and the figures for the high watermark of Egypt's liberal party. He knows too the turn-out in the election of 2012 and the exact percentage of Egyptians who voted for the presidency of Morsi.

In his articles he is a reporter from the front-line with a grasp of fine detail. When broadcasters of note are removed from their jobs on February 13th 2012 he names them: Hamdi Qandil, Ibrahim Eissa, Doaa Sultan, Dina Abdel Rahma. The citizen who is jailed for two years for a social media post is named as Bishwi Al-Buhairi. Massacres of the innocent are given their precise social geography. They took place in Maspero Square and Mohamed Mahmoud Street.

Al-Aswany has the advantage of his profession and the cosmopolitan element in his education. He knows that dictatorship is not something that is contained within the confines of the Presidential Palace. Its spread, he says, is everywhere like a cancer. Those subjected to its effects in turn become small dictators who mete out punishment and bullying to the less strong. Early in his working life his Department Head instructs him to go out and buy him a railway ticket to Alexandria. He declines: "Because I am a dentist, and not your office boy or your assistant." A teacher who has a doctorate in surgery carries out the chore instead. Al-Aswany leaves to study in the USA.

At the University of Illinois it is the practice that the graduates contribute a few dollars weekly to the communal coffee fund. The head of the Egyptian Students Union drinks a larger quantity of coffee and eats more snacks than the norm. He pays into the fund once or twice then stops altogether. The department secretary tries to approach him and he avoids her. Eventually when confronted his response is "Do you know who I am? I'm the head of the Egyptian Students Union; I'm a representative of Egypt. It's wrong of you to ask me to contribute. I won't tolerate it."

The American puts it to him that he must either pay or cease helping himself. In meeting Al-Aswany, his fellow Egyptian elevates the issue to the American woman being anti-Arab or anti-Islamic. The author's reply is that the quarrel has nothing to do with Egypt or Islam. "If there's anybody who brings shame on Arabs and Muslims", he says, "it is you and no-one else."

Democracy is deeply embedded in culture and, back in Egypt, he knows the difference of a state where it is not. He knows that Mubarak holds direct control over the judiciary. He makes comparison with France. His country's culture is "devoid of any real content". In a democracy an officer who issues a command, any command, is not "a national symbol". There is no notion such as the "prestige of the state". He observes in Egypt the working of a republic that is virtual. It has a parliament whose debate may appear vigorous but which has undergone official pre-approval.

Public language is understood by everyone as masquerade. "If the government claims that it won't raise the prices of oil, the people realise that the cheap oil will disappear so that they have to buy the expensive type anyway." The Ministry of Health issues a statement to the effect that there are no summer diseases. That is understood to mean that cholera is epidemic. Citizens are reported to have committed suicide while in custody. Without justice everyone understands that advancement is not based on competence. "Selfishness, negativity, hypocrisy and opportunism become predominant characteristics."

Al-Aswany looks back to history. In 1906 an incident occurred in the village of Denshawai between Egyptians and British officers. The trial that followed resulted in the hanging of four villagers and imprisonment for dozens of others. George Bernard Shaw wrote about the case. If the Empire meant a ruling as in Denshawai: "then there can be no more sacred and urgent political duty on earth than the disruption, defeat and suppression of the Empire." Unlike the present day in Egypt, Shaw received no accusation of being a traitor or of hostility to the army. In fact, Britain behaved in a way that was precisely opposite. The criticism of Denshawai led to the removal of Lord Cromer, the Consul-General.

His knowledge of history is full and dispassionately deployed. He refers to the first caliphs Abu Bakr and Umar Ibn Al-Khattab and the nationalist Ahmed Urabi of 1892. He cites the 1919 revolution and the showdown between the Wafd Party led by Saad Zaghlould and King Fuad I. The result was the constitution of 1923. The Muslim Brotherhood, historically, supported all of the autocratic rulers from King Farouk, Isma'il Sadqi, strongman of the Sha'ab Party, to Nasser and Sadat. Against the trend of other political actors, they participated in the elections called by Mubarak.

Of the Revolution he says simply it was "the greatest experience of my life". His report *Will you detain all Egypt?* has a grip that only participation can give. The gas thrown by the authorities came from three directions so that in their indifference it even hit their own police. The snipers who were deployed on rooftops could be identified by the white cloths worn on their heads against the sun. "In the evenings, the laser sights of their guns would circle the square and, when they stopped moving, a bullet would hit one of the demonstrators, blowing their head clean off." The writer as intellectual has knowledge of a psychology paper that he has found. In situations of revolution individuality is suppressed in favour of the collective endeavour.

But he notes sanguinely that so many of the servants of the former state remain in place. University and college deans and provincial governors are all implicated. Al-Aswany calls for their replacement with "independent, clean and honest people". He observes the sons, Gamal and Alaa Mubarak, coming out of a courtroom with Habib el-Adly, the former Minister of the Interior. They are not handcuffed but laughing together. The treatment given to the former minister by police and military is as if he were still in office. In his terms one hundred and sixty-five thousand "thugs" remain on the payroll of the security services, immune to arrest.

He has had lessons from his time in Illinois on power's limits. The interim Military Council in Cairo shows no differentiation between regime and state. A specific in art is interpreted as a general statement. When *The Yacoubian Building* is to be filmed, a complaint is lodged with the Egyptian Syndicate of Journalists. A journalist in his fiction is homosexual and it is interpreted to mean that all journalists are gay. He notes that the complaint is not upheld. But it is indicative. A bad doctor or a deviant lawyer in a television series is cause for calls to ban its showing.

He fights repeatedly against notions of the tribe. "Whereas democratic culture maintains responsibility lies with the individual", he says, "tribal mentality is based on the concept of collective responsibility." In this light all police are guilty of the crimes of a minority. All Copts are denounced by the religious Sheikhs for the actions of a few. "The principle of collective responsibility jeopardises the establishment of a modern nation."

The gulf between individual and collective is evident in the working of the Muslim Brotherhood. "The inherent problem with the Muslim Brotherhood is the distance between their moral rectitude as individuals and their political tractability as an organisation. Most of the Brothers are good and devoted people. When Morsi wins", Al-Aswany writes, "it is our duty to congratulate President Morsi, but it is also our duty to remind him of a few truths. He was not elected with Brotherhood votes alone, insufficient in number, but by millions of others." It is incumbent on him to "sever his ties with the Muslim Brotherhood immediately", in favour of a broad transitional government.

It does not happen. In September 2012, *How to Make a Dictator* states: "We expected the first elected post-revolution president to establish a real democracy, but unfortunately he kept in place the machinery of dictatorship that he inherited." In the background there is ever the influence of Saudi Arabia and its hidden funding, its purpose the promotion of Wahhabism and Salafism.

Al-Aswany attends a literary gathering in Paris. A demonstration is being held against him outside L'Institut du Monde Arabe. Inside he notices that only those in the back rows seem interested in the topic, his novel *The Egyptian Automobile Club*. Half an hour into the event a man stands up with the shout "We want to talk about Egypt." Others take off their shirts to reveal T-shirts with the four-finger rabia sign. This is a hand gesture of a raised palm with a bent thumb, symbol of protest. A French woman protests: "What you are doing is uncivilised. We came to a literary event to listen to an Egyptian author." She is punched in the face.

His opponents are hostile to all art. "The extremist mentality is, by nature, closed to any kind of imagination." He recounts the intolerance, the attacks and killings of Egypt's Christians, a community with a heritage that pre-dates the Prophet. He deplores the assaults on women and the misogyny whereby the onset of menstruation is synonymous with sexual activity. "A man can have intercourse with a ten-year-old girl as long as she can bear it" is his version of this theology. A response to theology has been dictated by the new authorities. Mosques have closed and preachers required to be registered. Sermons have been standardised and adapted to praise the government. But the expansion of the Suez Canal is officially a "gift from God". Lawsuits from the University of Al-Azhar continue against authors and artists on grounds of blasphemy.

Al-Aswany is a reporter from a polity in ferment but a society that is nonetheless vibrant in its inner life. He has no equivalent in the literary life of Britain. *The Egyptian Automobile Club* is a caustic allegory and a great novel. When he attends a gathering in Montreal he cites the Coptic Pope Shenouda III with a quotation that sums him up. "Egypt is not a country we live in but a country that lives in us."

January 2016: London

Doctor Dee and the Exemplar Number of All Things Numerable

The Royal College of Physicians is situated in the south-east corner of Regent's Park. Surrounded by cream stucco villas of the Thomas Cubitt era, the College's building had Dennis Lasdun as architect. Completed in 1964 it is Grade One listed. Like the National Theatre, three miles to the south and ten years later, its exterior is one of rectangles. Its interior is also one of light, open space and the use of multiple galleries. For the first six months of the year, this exhilarating space is host to a documentary exhibition dedicated to a famous medical predecessor, Doctor John Dee.

The Royal College is owner of more than one hundred of Dee's books. They were one of the greatest literary collections of the period. His long life spanned 1527 to1608 or 1609. The books are in glass cases, shielded from light by heavy cloth. Dee was adviser to Edward VI and Elizabeth I on subjects as various as navigation, astrology and health. His interests took in mathematics, natural history, music, astronomy, military history, cryptography and alchemy. In 1547 he met the map-maker Mercator in Louvain. The range of subjects he studied there included civil law "for recreation". In tackling history, he used mathematics to calculate details of the Greek fleet in the Trojan War.

John Dee was born in London to Rowland Dee and Johanna Wild. The name "Dee" derives from the Welsh word "du", pronounced "dee", meaning "black". His grandfather was called Bedo Ddu and came from Nant-y-groes, Pilleth in Radnorshire. John Dee constructed a pedigree showing his descent from Rhodri

21

the Great, Prince of Wales. The Dee family had come to London after the coronation of Henry Tudor as Henry VII. The son's formidable intellect saw him enter St John's College, Cambridge, in 1542 at the age of fifteen. He became a fellow of Trinity College, Cambridge, on its founding by Henry VIII in 1546. When he went on to lecture at Paris on Euclid, spectators wishing to hear clung to the windows. With his grasp of mathematics and astronomy he became an expert in navigation. He was important in training the seamen who were to give Britain command of the world's oceans.

Dee was at the heart of the Elizabethan state. An occasional advisor and tutor to the Queen he had close relationships with her ministers, Francis Walsingham and William Cecil. He tutored Sir Philip Sidney, Robert Dudley, 1st Earl of Leicester, and had the patronage of Sir Christopher Hatton. Dee has his counterparts in later times in Britain who persist into the present day. There is a small group of servants to the state who move frictionlessly between the Oxbridge apex and Whitehall. Their best fictional rendering is in the ten-novel sequence *Strangers and Brothers* by C P Snow. The books grew to be eagerly anticipated on their appearance over the years 1940-1970 and are now hardly read.

If the type persists, no modern figure is quite the like of Dee. To walk the light-filled space of the Royal College and follow the life and work is to look into the past via a pair of variable lenses. Through one his deeds are recognisable and understandable. Through the other he is a figure of misty strangeness and unknowability.

Science looks for conclusion based on observation. Theory in the Popperian consensus is only as good as its capacity for falsification. Matter has turned out to be a swirl of unseeable sub-parts. The quantum world proposes unpredictability. Dee the Renaissance polymath sought a totality of explanation. His modern interpreters debate whether his work was science or its obverse. While the captains of Britain's ships were beneficiaries of his practical work, Dee was as absorbed by the study of magic, astrology and Hermetic philosophy. For the last thirty years of his life he tried to commune with angels. They were the route to the universal language that underlay all creation. Dee made no distinction between mathematical research and divination and the summoning of angels. It was all one, the quest for understanding of the divine forms beneath the world of visible appearances. He was Plato's heir and he called the objects of his search "pure verities".

Through the windows of the Royal College the first snowdrops of the season can be seen in the park. The flowers outside are a distraction of predictability and allure from the words and pictures on the walls. The exhibits are a heady blend of biography, history and speculative philosophising. No creative mind is ever independent of its intellectual context. Pythagorean doctrines were pervasive in the Renaissance and Dee too believed numbers to be the basis of all phenomena. There was no concept of a division between the works of nature and the divine. Copernicus cited the mystic Hermes Trismegistus. In his theory of elliptical orbits Kepler attempted to confirm Pythagorean concepts of cosmic harmony. Tycho Brahe wrote treatises on the astrological significance of his astronomy.

At one level Dee the man connects across the centuries. His acquisition of intellectual mastery was achieved through self-discipline. At Cambridge he divided his day rigorously with four hours for sleep and two hours for meals. That left eighteen in the day for work. From his house on the Thames at Mortlake he watched the moon in eclipse in 1556 and 1566. He entertained with gusto, his guests including Sir Walter Raleigh, the Earl of Leicester, and the geographer Abraham Ortelius. The French ambassador Michel de Castelnau introduced him to Jean Bodin in 1581. Where he enters into spheres which are beyond the present-day visitor to this exhibition he can still be appreciated. But the appreciation is for aesthetic rather than cognitive reasons.

The psychological truth of Gestalt, that perception seeks a whole, is universal. In that respect Dee vaults across the divide of time. True to Pythagoras, he discerns the relatedness of mathematics and music. The universe becomes a metaphor of "a lyre tuned by some excellent artificer, whose strings are separate species of the universal whole." There is no gap between enquiry and authority: "Wonderful things can be performed truly and naturally without violence to faith in God or injury to the Christian religion."

It is the gift of the natural philosopher to know how to touch the strings of the great lyre "dexterously and make them vibrate would bring forth marvellous harmonies." Dee's goal was utterly sensible. All the branches of natural philosophy, as he wrote in his *Monas Hieroglyphica* of 1564, asked for attention. Optics, alchemy, astrology, mathematics, geometry and astronomy were all awaiting their unification. It was a book that proved difficult to read. The keenest royal in Europe, Rudolf II in Prague, confessed it too hard and beyond him.

Numbers are crucial in Dee's schema for the intermediary role that they perform between the natural and supernatural levels of the cosmos. The highest and most abstract state of number is reserved for the Creator. The intermediary level is to be found in "Spiritual and Angelical myndes and in the Soule of man". Dee's preference for speculation over empiricism was based on his epistemological acceptance of scripture. The natural world was inherently uncertain owing to its corruptible and changeable nature. It was the supernatural that provided the natural philosopher with certainty and truth. In this duality there was no value to observation or experiment.

In that sense, he is remotely of the past and far away from us. But instead his words are still possessed of alluring qualities. In the *Mathematical Preface* he wrote that numbers "may both winde and draw our selves into the inward and deep search and view, of all creatures distinct vertues, natures, properties, and Formes: and also, farder, arise, clime, ascend, and mount up (with Speculative winges) in spirit, to behold in the Glas of Creation, the Forme of Formes, the Exemplar Number of all things Numerable: both visible and invisible: mortall and immortall Corporall and Spirituall."

Dee is not so far from the mathematicians of our age. Herman Weyl: "If the transcendental is only accessible to us through the medium of images and symbols, let the symbols at least be as distinct and as unambiguous as mathematics will permit." Dee jumps the centuries. His word-craft is as seductive as his delight with his calling. "O comfortable, allurement, O ravishing perswasion to deal with a Science whose subject is so Auncient", he writes, "so pure, so excellent, so surmounting all creatures, so used of the Almighty and incomprehensible wisdom of the Creator, in the creation of all creatures." Doctor Dee is an enthusiast. The conjunction at this time, the first yielding of winter, is a nice one. A world without snowdrops in bud would be one that gave less joy. But a world without Doctor Dee, and his kind, would equally be one bereft of another beauty, the gravity of spirit.

January 2016: London

A Liberal Retrospective

No family has had an impact on the lands of the Rivers Dyfi and Upper Severn to equal that of the Davies dynasty. The first David Davies brought the railway in its boom age of the nineteenth century from Shropshire to the sea. The village of Derwenlas had been a small port. The building of the railway over bog land removed the water from its edge. The cutting made by Davies' engineers and builders through the hill at Talerddig was for decades the deepest in the world.

The next generations expanded the impact from engineering into cultural life. In Aberystwyth the Old Library with its curlicue Art Nouveau signage has a plaque carved in stone. "This stone", it states, "was laid by David Davies Esq, J P of Plas Dinam Mont Friday, July 28th 1905." At the outset of the First World War, one and a half million refugees came to Britain from Belgium. The Davies home of Gregynog had long been a place of music and composers of Belgium found there a wartime refuge. In 2014 a concert of their music was held in Aberystwyth in centenary honour.

Aberystwyth University was the first in the world to create a specific Department of International Politics. Within it is located the David Davies Memorial Institute whose annual lecture has brought over the years a series of speakers from the peaks of government and political scholarship. The lectures began in 1954 and the present Lord and Lady Davies are seated in the third row of the Department's packed main hall. The guest is William Wallace, Baron Wallace of Saltaire.

Wallace was created a life peer in December 1995. Liberals are close to Europe. In 1997 he became a member of the Select Committee on the European Communities as well as Chairman of the Sub-Committee on Justice and Home Affairs. In 2001 he became the Liberal Democrats' main frontbencher on foreign affairs in the House of Lords. On the formation of the Westminster coalition in 2010 he became a government whip and spokesperson in the Lords for the Foreign and Commonwealth Office, the Department for Work and Pensions and the Department for Education. His work prior to parliament spanned academic institutions and thinktanks in teaching and board roles. The Royal Institute of International Affairs, the London School of Economics, Manchester University, St Antony's College at Oxford and the Central European University have all been parts of his past. Visiting roles as a fellow or professor have taken him to the USA, Germany, France, Italy, Greece and Belgium. He has fought five parliamentary elections. He was candidate for Huddersfield West in 1970, Manchester Moss Side in the two elections of 1974, and fought the Shipley constituency in 1983 and 1987.

The audience for the David Davies Memorial Institute lecture is primarily young. For them Wallace's work for the Liberal party is the stuff of history. In 1966 he was the Liberals' Assistant Press Officer working on behalf of the leader, Jo Grimond. He worked as a speechwriter for David Steel. He was co-author of the 1979 Liberal election manifesto. During the time of the alliance between the Liberals and the Social Democratic Party, 1982-87, he was a member of the joint party steering committee. He was co-author of the 1997 election manifesto for the renamed Liberal Democrats. Wallace is steeped in a half-century of politics and his lecture is a journey into history. His title is *Losing the Narrative: Europe and the United Kingdom*.

Wallace's audience belongs in the main to the generation that has never known anything other than open movement across the nations of Europe. Hilary Benn, Shadow Foreign Secretary, is campaigning emphatically across Britain for retention of membership of the European Union. The week previously he too has been in front of a young audience, this occasion in London. For those who have never known it, Benn evoked the period that preceded Britain's accession. Wallace too touches on early memories of travel as a young man. He too mentions the quarter of an hour wait at a Dover customs checkpoint and the same again at Boulogne. A small brigade of Customs Officers marked with sticks of chalk the suitcases as they passed their scrutiny. In fact, he underestimates the time that it took a family car to enter via Dover. It took far longer than a quarter of an hour.

Migration is an issue in the nascent debates on Europe. It is, Wallace reminds his audience, a journey in two directions. Less is to be heard from, or about, the myriads of Britons who work across Europe. Wallace recounts a meeting at the Home Office. The Department is characteristically sharp on the numbers of non-British citizens within the borders of its jurisdiction. Information on its opposite, the number of Britons making use of their privilege to work across Europe, is elusive. Wallace has pursued the numbers. At least ten thousand Britons, he states, are beneficiaries of Germany's welfare system.

Hilary Benn was born in 1953, Wallace a decade earlier in 1941. To come from that era is to be aware of the conditions that ignited the urge for a different Europe. Wallace recalls the generation of politicians whose outlook had been forged in active military service. Just as Clement Attlee had been at Gallipoli the generation of Dennis Healey, Lord Carrington and William Whitelaw had all seen military action. They were political leaders whose formative experience had been European failure. Three times in seventy years, Wallace reminds his audience, France and Germany had gone to war. He has even brought with him a book by David Davies as evidence of the urge for something better and more enduring.

Nations, like individuals, are sustained by narratives about themselves. Britain's self-storying has changed rapidly. In the frame of historical time the descent from the triumphalism of 1945 to the sense of economic feebleness was dramatically swift. Solution was seen in adherence to the young European Economic Community. David Cornwell is the real name of John le Carré. Before becoming the master chronicler of the Cold War he was on the staff of the British Embassy in Germany. In Bonn he witnessed the early attempts by the Prime Minister to win German support for Britain's joining the then grouping of six nations.

Wallace goes back to where it began. Churchill made his speech of September 19th 1946 in Zurich. Within Britain the turnaround of Labour has been dramatic. Much of it was due to the tenure of Roy Jenkins at the Presidency. Wallace recalls the transformative address of Jacques Delors to the 1978 Conference of the Trades Unions Council. The single market of 1992 was the radical change, with the Britain of Mrs Thatcher its keenest advocate. Labour had long been suspicious of the three "C"'s of the EEC. In its first days it was Capitalist, Conservative and Catholic. The suspicions of Labour, as evidenced in the strong and regular advocacy of its Shadow Foreign Secretary, have long since dissipated.

The productivity gap between Britain and the Continent has been perennial, subject of government concern and attention for a half century. In 2016 it is symptom of a bifurcated Britain. The productivity of London and the South-east is the equal of Europe. The national average is pulled down by the economics of the outside regions. In the middle ages the wealth of Britain split hugely across the line from the Severn Estuary to the Wash. Britain has again separated between south and north. The term "Northern Powerhouse" Wallace dismisses as public relations sloganising. But the peer from Saltaire and Shipley has anxiety about the separation of London from the bulk of the territory that it dominates. He is persuasive. In the liberal order thirty-one thousand properties in the capital are in the ownership of offshore companies. Economic analysis has it that this proportion is so low as to have no effect on the remainder of the capital's housing stock. But it feels wrong. Swathes of windows on a winter walk by night through the streets of Kensington and Westminster are unlit. Their owners are as much ghosts as those who have claimed the terraces of Abersoch and Llanbedrog.

Not everything that Wallace says convinces. It is a shibboleth of opposition belief that war impelled the Conservatives to victory in the election of 1983. The consensus from the psephologists is that the election was for the government to win without any boost from the Falklands. Single-factor political determinants are nice in their simplicity of explanation but they rarely hold up to a depth of scrutiny. The polls on Europe are already charting out the gulf in attitude between the generations. Wallace's mainly youthful audience has after all known no other polity.

* * * *

Wallace is visitor to a Liberal Party redoubt of Britain. Even in the General Election of 2015 Ceredigion delivered a three thousand vote lead. If the party was decimated across swathes of Britain Wallace's presence is a reminder that Liberalism remains a force in the Lords. The party itself like all parties is a coalition. Nick Clegg is a bloodied practitioner. "Parties", he writes, "only win by appealing to a broad range of local opinion within their constituencies." Clegg identifies a stream of strands drawn to the party. At one end of the spectrum of ideology are classical free-market supporters. They rub shoulders with foreign policy interventionists and community-centred social democrats.

Dig beneath the surface and humanists jostle with non-conformist Christians, repairers of potholes with intellectual radicals. The durability of Liberalism with a capital "L" is as much its strength as its historic record is a rallying cry. But a term of political philosophy that has lasted has only done so by embracing elasticity. Elasticity can also be a sign of a tensile strength. It has certainly a durability with which Labourism cannot compete. But then Labourism, a term that exists but is hardly used, has no "neo" attached to it for use as a general term of contempt and insult.

The word itself, Liberalism, was first noted in 1819. The future railway-builder of Wales and creator of the port of Barry, David Davies was then a one-year-old infant. Over nearly two centuries it has at different times meant different things. The first political liberals to use the name were Spaniards who opposed the king's suspension of the constitution in 1814. The word spread from Spain to France. But it dug deepest in Britain with its philosophical exponent in John Stuart Mill. In journalism, James Wilson, a Liberal member of Parliament, founded its house newspaper *The Economist*. That strand looked to the freedom of individuals and markets within the jurisdiction of a state with clear limits.

That is not how it is understood elsewhere. In the Mediterranean countries it has a meaning wholly different and exactly opposite to its use in America. There it is associated with big rather than limited government, its starting-point Franklin D Roosevelt and the New Deal. Across the southern flank of the European Union, it is hallmark of a global order presided over by the World Bank and the International Monetary Fund. Elsewhere again the word seems to be bereft of any consistent meaning at all. In Japan, the Liberal Democratic Party is mildly conservative and nationalist. Russia has a party of the same name that is utterly opposed to liberal tenets. Canada shares with Britain a Liberal Party where name and philosophy are attuned. In some countries the name has been abandoned. In Denmark, the Venstre party occupies a position on the liberal centre-right. In France, all names are up for grabs.

The word has a shared etymology with "liberty" and "liberation". In the countries of wealth the discourse has shifted. The environment is the province of green parties. Politicians who prioritise privacy occupy all parties. If liberalism is elusive its opposites are not. Authoritarianism and fundamentalism are much discussed and combatted but the concept of Single-Issue-Solutionism, just as enticing, is not. Liberalism is better interpreted in Wittgensteinian terms of possessing family resemblances. Progress is there along with a scepticism towards authority, respect for individuals, a separation of powers within sovereignty.

Liberals themselves are a feature of the history of France and Germany as much as in the Anglosphere. François Guizot, the French statesman and historian, is one of their number. Before Lord Acton he voiced the liberal conviction that power corrupts. In Germany Franz Hermann Schulze-Delitzsch founded the first credit unions. When Labour won its tenth election its leader acknowledged Liberals as predecessors to what he represented. "My heroes aren't just Ernie Bevin, Nye Bevan and Attlee", Tony Blair declared, "they are also Keynes, Beveridge, Lloyd George." He went on to make the link between social-democratic progressivism with radicalism. "Division among radicals almost one hundred years ago resulted in a 20th century dominated by Conservatives", he said. "I want the 21st century to be the century of the radicals." So it has turned out to be, but not in the way he intended. The words of Blair do not carry much public weight.

Certainly, the liberal inheritance in Britain is formidable. Trade unions were legalised in 1871 under Liberal Prime Minister William Gladstone. His government introduced the Representation of the People Act 1884, whereby the right to vote jumped to sixty per cent of male adults. The Education Act of 1870 established schooling for all children between the ages of five and twelve. Gladstone himself was a classic individualist

Liberal advocating low taxes and a minimal state. But welfarist, cooperative and redistributive strains were part of liberalism's bloodstream. John Stuart Mill supported taxes on unearned income, inheritance taxes, trade unions, worker co-operatives, participatory democracy, votes for women as well as men.

Liberalism has always understood social obligation to transcend self-interest. The tension between individualist and welfarist strands was illustrated in Gladstone's resignation in 1894. Its prompting was in part his opposition to the proposal by his Liberal chancellor Sir William Harcourt to introduce death duties. This division led to its cataclysmic defeat in the 1895 general election. A revived Liberal Party was back with a huge election victory in 1906 which went on to lay the foundations of the welfare state. The state pension, compulsory health insurance, unemployment and sickness pay and an extension of free secondary education had in them the hand of David Lloyd George.

William Beveridge moved from sympathy with the Fabians toward the Liberals, and was a Liberal MP from 1944-1945. His *Beveridge Report* of 1942 was the template for the post-war government. Labour's social policy was as indebted to liberal ideas as its economic policy was to Keynesian notions of full employment. Now the debates have shifted. The triumph of medicine has been astonishing but the expectation of decades of pensionable non-working life has thrown up policy issues that have never existed before. If Lord Wallace and modern liberalism stand for anything it goes back to the Enlightenment and the application of reason. That itself has the capacity to be radical since its antagonists include convention and myth. It is still combative because it is not awed by custom or hierarchy. It still knows that power without interruption corrupts and privilege perpetuates itself. Most of all it knows dispute and argument to be not just inevitable but indispensable for the vitality of institutions. Liberalism's greatest strength is its capacity to reinvent itself.

Back in the university hall, the vote of thanks is given by the Director of the David Davies Memorial Institute. He is a graduate of Charles University in Prague. Scholarship is borderless. The audience includes young people from Hamburg and Frankfurt, beneficiaries of the Union's Erasmus Programme. Cross-border student flows and collaborative research funds are the lifeblood of the universities. Wallace is on friendly soil. The benefits of Union are so manifest as to be untested. Questions are asked but they never doubt the wisdom or the continuity of union. Wallace points to the likes of the low-cost airlines as example of the benefits of European-derived liberalism. An alternative to the status quo that has prevailed for forty years is in this context, a gathering of the privileged, inconceivable.

February 2016: Aberystwyth

We Became Orphans:
A Writer in the Yucatan

Eaton Square in London's Belgravia is a place of privilege. It always has been although in the past it was privileged in a different way. It was once home to actors and singers. Sean Connery and Robin Gibb have lived here. A plaque on number eighty marks it as the home of Victorian philanthropist George Peabody. Prime Minister Stanley Baldwin lived at number eighty-six, Count Metternich at number forty-four.

I have once been inside a home not in Eaton Square itself, but just around the corner. A fifth-floor flat of some opulence in a mansion block was not my usual haunt but the tenant was a friend of a friend and a relative of the owner. The owner himself was a City player who had featured in the press. Dispute over his role in a secondary bank collapse had led him to flee to a permanent life on his yacht off Antibes. Such figures were always a part of London's make-up. Eaton Square is now part of the new London although it has lost its famous actors and singers. The building improvements are incessant. Crews of Polish builders cluster on the pavement for their cigarette break. Dachshunds and Shih Tzus are exercised by domestic staff from the Philippines.

By day the Polish builders and the Filipino dog-walkers are all the human life on the street. By night there is hardly a lit-up front room to be seen. The quarters for the domestics and the caretakers are to the rear or dug deep beneath the ground. It is an improbable, empty zone for my visit by darkness, but one window is brightly lit and its door is ajar in welcome to strangers. The Square is home to the London branch of the Instituto Cervantes. The Institution's guest speaker on this winter night is John Harrison, author of books on Antarctica and also Latin America. For his most recent journey he has left the high Andes and travelled in Mexico. His book's title is *1519: A Journey to the End of Time* and is the subject of his talk.

Travel writing lives or dies by the openness of the ear and the acuity of the eye. Harrison shows a photograph of a sheet of placid water. It looks unremarkable, at least to the audience member in the second row. But Harrison on the podium can read water with a sharper eye. A subtle change in watery tone says it all. A lesser penetration of the bright Mexican sunlight into the water is indicator that a sandbar is present. Harrison has taken his photograph on the coast of the Yucatan. His lens sees what the Conquistadors saw, recognising the water as threat. Harrison's journey of today has followed that of Hernan Cortes of 1519.

By this time on their voyage the adventurers on Spain were low on fresh water. The lurking sandbars and the lack of harbours along the coast of the Yucatan necessitated that the shore be approached in small boats. That in turn meant exposure to danger from the host population. On a map the route that Cortes took to the Aztec capital, the island city of Tenochtitlan, follows a strange and straggling course. Its principal motivation, explains Harrison, had been the avoidance of hazard. The Yucatan and the interior of Mexico were a patchwork of peoples and political groupings in a framework of alliances.

The colonists in the Belgravia of today are as much new arrivals as were the Spaniards in sixteenth-century Mexico but there is a difference. Their nominee companies in the Cayman Islands are the discreet holders of great wealth from elsewhere. A new tourist trip in London calls itself the Kleptocracy Tour. Its passengers travel the most gilded streets and squares of London and the tour guide names the owners of glitzy properties. The Conquistadors, by contrast, came from the most arid regions of their home country. They sought wealth and the Americas had silver. Its extraction for shipment to Madrid and, at a later stage, in bulk to the Bank of England wrecked the Spanish currency.

Journeying is encounter and Harrison's is filled with the cheer he takes in the company of the inhabitants of present-day Mexico. The countryside is deep in historical texture. The cultural authorities have listed twenty-seven thousand sites of historical and archaeological note. The Maya developed a mathematics of extraordinary beauty and invention. In the art of Rivera, Orozco and Siqueiros the country's Revolution unleashed a public declarative art that has no equivalent elsewhere. Harrison himself sees Rivera murals in Tlaxcala's town hall. He visits the high points of Maya culture, like the frescos of Bonampak with their barely-dimmed luminous blues. But his central theme is the collision of Spain with the states which prevailed across the Atlantic, an encounter that was merciless and relentless.

Harrison has previously written of the spectrum of the hues of blue in the Polar Regions. The steamy heat of Vera Cruz in this book could not be a greater climatic contrast but he is ever alive to the movement and colour around him. At his starting-point on the tip of the Yucatan peninsula he calls it "the anvil on which the Caribbean beats". He writes of the frigate birds that fly by at eye level, with their wing length greater than any avian species other than the largest albatross. He relishes the colours of the region's fine pottery, the composition of the soils providing contrasts of black with ochre and black with russet.

He has prepared for Mexico itself with a visit to the home territory of the Conquistadors. Extremadura in Spain is the harshest of European landscapes. Harrison visits Medellin and Trujillo, the home of the brothers Pizarro, the conquerors of the Incas. He looks to the great historian Fernand Braudel to emphasise just how harsh was this area that forged the adventurers of imperial Spain. Much of Europe had barely enough soil of the requisite quality to provide food for its cities. The trees in this region of Spain were long gone and the introduction of three million Merino sheep by 1450 was a disaster of soil erosion. From this context of life on the edge it is small surprise that the assault on Mexico was so total. Two Maya were seized early on for use as translators. But first they were baptised. Their original names are unknown and history knows them only as Julian and Melchior.

Harrison is alert to the persistence of the pre-Colombian culture. The city of Puebla now is home to a vast Volkswagen plant but the remoter southern states are still rooted in kin and group. Catholicism sits astride beliefs that stretch back millennia. To enter a church like that of Chamula in Chiapas is to be in a world of utter theological strangeness. "Look in a hotel mirror", Harrison writes, "and the world seems much like any other Latin country. Look in a Native obsidian mirror; panther-dark figures are behind you in the room."

Harrison remembers writers who have gone before. Bernal Diaz was a member of the first expedition and on arrival in Yucatan was aged around twenty-four. He was a soldier but also a writer and without him, says Harrison, "our picture of the human contact between these two worlds would usually remain monochrome. He can make it blaze into colour." Later Mexico's Day of the Dead puts him in mind of Malcolm Lowry in Cuernavaca. He is sceptical about Graham Greene.

When he raises his book for a first reading he homes in on a ruin. The Baja Iglesia is a hunk of stone wall whose present-day inhabitants are fruit bats. They are a species that lends itself to the symbolism. Their habit of nipping fruit made them into a symbol for decapitation. His sprightly reading of this passage ends with a shock sentence: "I was supposed to be dead."

John Harrison's journey is in fact a double one. Mexico is interspersed with hellish journeys that take him no more than a couple of miles from his London home. The food of the country is succulent. In Puebla the speciality dish comes drenched in a mix of chili and bitter chocolate. At the ruins of El Tajin he records that half his calorie intake is comprised of guacamole and milk flavoured with vanilla. Tortillas and rice without an abundance of sauce are beyond him. The reason is a shortage of saliva and a protective mucous that wraps itself around food of any solidity.

Threaded between the writer's reactions to Cabo Catoche, Champoton and Campeche are accounts of visits to St Mary's Hospital in Paddington. Facial expression is contained in the muscles around the eye and in the cheek. On the stage at the Instituto Cervantes Harrison is a vital presence. His eyes have the sparkle of absorption in his theme but his face is bereft of what might be spare flesh. His jacket hangs over a frame of bone. Throat cancer and its treatment have left in their wake the impression of a body scraped of all surface that is inessential.

This parallel journey has started in a location as unthreatening as a street in Bayswater. The pavement has taken on the texture of a slack trampoline and he collapses. Harrison's first remedy is swift in the form of two pints of bitter. It happens a second time and a Chinese-Australian doctor asks: "Have you noticed any discharge from your nipples?" Tests and scans follow. A shadow the size of a walnut reveals itself, the most optimistic interpretation that it is a cyst filled with liquid. Later at Rhosygilwen Mansion in Pembrokeshire for a speaking event his voice is weak and a mild sore throat persists. The doctors rule out tuberculosis and an endoscopy follows. Two small nodules at the back of the tongue are revealed. Fine needles through his neck pull out cell samples.

Throat cancer at the author's age has associations with the drinking of spirits, smoking or a history of syphilis or septicaemia. His score is none out of four. The condition is treatable but not operable. Of the shadow at the tongue's base he notices: "they always talk of treatment, not cure". He knows his John Donne and the cancer patient with a low probability of survival writes: "I look across the deadly waters ... separating me from the main." He knows his Kuebler-Ross too and remembers a Pontcanna drinking companion with the same diagnosis.

The course of his treatment is given in unremitting harshness. "Fear is under control. I find I am content and almost happy", he is able to say. But radiation treatment and chemotherapy in parallel are appalling. He shrinks physically, even his feet, so that his shoes grow too large. "Weetabix with banana tastes like brake-pads soaked in battery acid", he writes. He wonders on his own probable end in time. In the park he sees the squirrels and thinks they may have more years of life ahead than he. It is a late-stage diagnosis which means a high radiation dosage. It burns and constricts the throat. His saliva glands barely function and mucous forms to protect the wound. He is dependent on a powdered food supplement. That in Mexico leads to the no-tortilla, guacamole and a milk-vanilla diet.

The treatment works at a cost. A tube in the stomach leaves a sunken scar hole. After two years food of any substance is still trapped in the mucous and is unswallowable. But he remembers Dennis Potter at Hay seeing his last Spring. The plum tree outside his window was "the whitest, frothiest, blossomest blossom there could ever be." Harrison looks to Shakespeare's Ariel. "Merrily, merrily shall I live now, Under the Blossom that hangs on the bough." He has washboard ribs but he looks at the trees of Bayswater in passing. They are racing into flower and, like them, he lives.

* * * *

The conquest by soldiers of Europe of the societies in the New World was settled by sword, horse, realpolitik, organisation, the drive of self-belief and the moral rightness of imperial expansion.

To the Americans the invaders were "monstrous marine animals, bearded men who moved upon the sea in large houses". But Europe had an unknown ally on its side. Just as Harrison's depleted self is turned into a biological and molecular battlefield, so too it was in the Americas. In that battle the losers had the bad fortune to be nature's victims. Over the hundred years from 1650 to 1750 the population of Europe, with Russia included, rose from one hundred and three million to one hundred and forty-four million. In South America it fell from twelve to eleven million. In Panama alone the death toll was upward of two million between 1514 and 1530.

The susceptibility of the Americans to premature death by natural causes was noted almost immediately by the arrivals from Europe. The Spaniards' first historian, Bartolomé de Las Casas, saw the illnesses as originating in the devil. With no knowledge of selective susceptibility he feared the worst. "A mortal pestilence which consumed these peoples", he wrote, "invented by Satan and all his ministers and officials to drag the Spaniards down into hell and all Spain to destruction."

Seventeen epidemics swept Mexico and Peru between 1520 and 1600. It was the same where the Portuguese ruled. In 1552 respiratory disease broke out around Pernambuco. In the same decade eight hundred inhabitants of a Mission at Rio de Janeiro died. In 1558 pleurisy and flux swept the coast from Rio to Espirito Santo. In 1558 smallpox arrived in Rio de la Plata and killed tens of thousands. The Portuguese were unscathed. A German missionary in 1699 wrote: "The Indians die so easily that the bare look and smell of a Spaniard causes them to give up the ghost." Antonio de Herrera, author of a multi-volume history at the beginning of the seventeenth century, observed that the Americans were aware of the invulnerability of the Spaniards. They kneaded blood into the bread they made for their new masters. Corpses were put into wells to no effect.

Unknown conditions appeared. In 1520 a devastating epidemic hit the Cakchiquel people of Guatamala; its main symptom was unstoppable nosebleeds. The Spanish triumph was helped by the shattering of political structures by disease. Toribio Motolinio wrote that "more than one half of the population died ... they died in heaps, like bedbugs." Montezuma's nephew Cuitlahuac became Lord of Mexico due to his uncle's death from smallpox. Peru was an absolute autocracy and Huayna Capac died. Cieza de Leon wrote that the mourning "was such that the lamentations and shrieks rose to the skies, causing the birds to fall to the ground."

Smallpox was the most deadly of the biological arrivals. For an unprotected population the death rate is around thirty percent. When it came to Iceland in 1707, eighteen thousand died within two years, out of a population of fifty thousand. Before Cortes even arrived in Mexico, smallpox was already raging. Spaniards had been shipwrecked on the coast of Yucatan in 1511. An expedition by Hernández de Córdoba sailed along the coast in 1517. Its arrival most likely came via Santa Domingo or Cuba. Bishop Diego de Landa was present to write "a pestilence seized them, characterised by great pustules, which rotted their bodies with a great stench, so that the limbs fell to pieces in four or five days."

Where the Spaniards and Portuguese had led the English followed. In 1585 Sir Francis Drake landed at the Cape Verde Islands. His crew picked up a highly contagious fever, most likely typhus, and transported it to the Caribbean and Florida. At St Augustine "the wilde people died verie fast and said among themselves, it was the Inglisshe God that made them die so faste" wrote an observer, Thomas Hariot. 1587 was the date of the English colony at Roanoke Island. Long before, fishermen and fur traders had landed on the Atlantic coast of Canada. The result was depopulation. A report by Jesuits in 1616 said that the peoples "are astonished and often complain that, since the French mingle with and carry on trade with them, they are dying fast and the population is thinning out."

In 1616 epidemic swept through New England. Cotton Mather observed that the woods were cleared "of those pernicious creatures, to make room for better growth." Whatever the disease may have been, those of European origin were immune. At the time of the Pilgrim Landing the tribe that inhabited the area of Plymouth Bay was almost completely exterminated by nature. In Boston Bay it was the same. Those who survived fled so that, as a witness wrote: "Carkases ly above the ground without burial ... And the bones and skulls upon the several places of their habitations made such a spectacle after my coming into those partes, that, as I travelled in the Forrest, nere the Massachusetts, it seemed to me a new found Golgotha." In the far-off north of the Americas Russian traders were the unknowing cause of death for thousands of Aleuts, Eskimos and Tlingits.

The biological invasion was not just microscopic. Seeds came in mud, dung and the folds of textiles. Daisies, dandelions, Kentucky bluegrass were among hundreds of new species. Whole fields in the Americas were colonised by plants unknown in the continent before 1492. Belief in the workings of the Divine was never far behind. Francisco de Aguilar, a Dominican friar, observed divine help. "When the Christians were exhausted from war, God saw fit to send the Indians smallpox, and there was great pestilence."

The assault of biology continued. At the end of the nineteenth century measles wreaked havoc in Tierra del Fuego. The anopheles mosquito arrived in Brazil from Africa around 1929. Its death toll was twenty thousand. In this unequal trade only the chigger and trepanoma pallidum passed in the other direction. The second invader grew in England and Wales to be second only to tuberculosis among infectious diseases as a cause of death. But it was a small strike on the part of nature. The true record was written by an observer from the Maya. He recorded: "Great was the stench of the dead ... The dogs and vultures devoured the bodies. The mortality was terrible. Your grandfathers died, and with them died the son of the king and his brothers and kinsmen. So it was that we became orphans. All of us were thus. We were born to die!"

As for the self-declared "servant of the high and mighty kings of Castile and Leon, civilisers of barbarous nations, their messenger and captain", Cortes caught dysentery and died of pleurisy aged sixty-two. His will requested that his remains be buried in Mexico. His body was moved repeatedly for different reasons. On the country's independence in 1823 his bones were hidden and only rediscovered in November 1946. They were moved again and laid for a final time beneath a bronze inscription and his coat of arms. Even in the twentieth century Cortes remained a symbol of cultural schism. An indigenous voice called for his bones to be burnt before an Aztec statue and for the ashes to be scattered in the air.

February 2016: London

A Visit to the Cloud

The Cloud is a brand name for a Sky subsidiary and a generic description for much of the world's data processing. Its origin as a term is uncertain. One theory is that it came from a traditional schematic whereby a circle, representing a server, was surrounded by other overlapping circles in a network diagram. As an image, it resembled a cloud.

Its use in print to refer to platforms for distributed computing can be traced back to an article in 1994 in the magazine *Wired*. The topic was a spin-off from Apple that had a distributed programming language, Telescript. In the article 'Bill and Andy's Excellent Adventure II' the author Andy Hertzfeld wrote about "the beauty of Telescript is that now, instead of just having a device to program, we now have the entire Cloud out there, where a single program can go and travel to many different sources of information and create sort of a virtual service." A reference to "cloud computing" in its now usual sense debuted in the industry in a 1996 document from Compaq. It takes a veteran memory to recall Compaq, a once brilliant tech star.

Internet statistics are out-of-date the day after they are issued. It took a while before the Internet attracted the attention of environmentalists. But when its electricity needs passed two percent of total world energy consumption, it did so. It was not just the figure itself that irked the environmental activists but the unstoppable upward curve. Its power usage was jumping upward at around twelve percent a year. The Cloud had fluffy, harmless associations. Like the phrase "Server Farm", it sounded good. An association with belching coal-fired power stations in the form of the "Dirty Cloud" was not what the tech industry relished.

The first data centres were located on traditional sites. An anonymous wall encloses a significant location in Newport, Gwent. Next Generation Data is a beneficiary of the great Lucky Goldstar project, signed off in 1996 by then Secretary of State William Hague, which never came about. Next Generation is Europe's leading provider of "premium carrier-neutral co-location data centres". Across the Atlantic the Network Access Point of the Americas is situated in Miami and dates back to 2001. It is substantial but not colossal, six floors encompassing seventy thousand square metres. Power in a climate like that of Florida is not just environmentally offensive but costs. The issue of distance is of low priority for these centres, certainly less by far than proof against flood, earthquake, service interruption or political tremor. The new titans of tech have changed the rules of the industry.

The social media goliath has four data centres at home, in Texas, Iowa, North Carolina and Oregon. The giant of search and advertising also has an installation on the mighty Columbus River in Oregon. The location has the advantages of remoteness, protectability and water in excess. Similar criteria were adopted when Facebook came to create its first hub outside the USA. Luleå is in the north of Sweden, two hundred kilometres from the Arctic Circle. The company states that it is the most energy-efficient computing facility yet to be built. It comes with the advantage of a winter average temperature of minus twenty centigrade. The freezing outside air is pumped into the centre as nature's coolant.

Electricity and its reliability count. Sweden's north has a power surplus. The system of hydroelectric dams was built for steel, iron ore, pulp and paper, industries whose demand has declined. Consumption for a site may be as big as for a steel mill but Facebook's goal is that its data centres be fifty percent powered by clean and renewable energy by 2018. It is not alone in the far

Scandinavian North. Hamina in Finland is the site for a Google complex.

These centres are the nodes of data's global nervous system. They have a tendency to slip off digital maps. Lob an enquiry into a search engine and the answers lean towards the vague and elusive. They need protection. The Network of the Americas in Miami has walls eighteen centimetres thick and doors of steel against earthquake shock. The service provider Datalis-Radix has made a data centre in Switzerland from a former military bunker encased within a mountain. Its fifteen thousand square feet on three levels date back to before the Second World War. The year of its decommissioning as a military centre is classified information. Access is via a door of steel that weighs twenty tonnes. These former military installations have an advantage of back-up power in case of conflict destroying the public supply. Two vast diesel generators are ever ready for switch-over in an emergency. It has a natural advantage of two aquifers and a natural spring which are sufficient to meet the cooling needs in addition to the temperature that prevails deep within its rock casing.

The numbers for data are so huge as to be outside comprehension. The largest exchange averages three and a half thousand gigabytes a second. In 2012, the total flows were two and a half quintillion bytes a day – the number has eighteen zeros. Four years later and the monthly flow has passed a Zettabyte – that is one followed by twenty-one zeroes, or sixteen billion 64-gigabyte smartphones. With artificial intelligence and machine learning the demand is greater by a new degree. Self-driving cars will generate one hundred gigs of data a second. At a low estimate computing capacity is still doubling every five years. But one number is invariable. The managers may ski to work in the near-Arctic north but there are few human beings around. Ironically the most skilled staff members are probably old-fashioned electrical engineers. Securing the unimpeded flow of electrical current is the number one task. The second largest cohort of staff is quite likely security. The need for carbon middleware is not great. "Carbon middleware" is how the engineers refer to themselves. The tech guys have their own instinct for humour.

* * * *

On this chilly February day I am below ground, my eyes fifteen inches from the lines of racks that make one small artery in this giant global flow. The servers are secured inside locked cages and behind plastic curtains that blow slightly in the air conditioner wind. There is no natural water or Arctic winter here. In England these eight-foot-high stacks of flashing digital system have instead air conditioners all around that blast continuously. Each rack, whose numbers run to hundred upon hundred, exudes the heat of an electric fire. The processors themselves have a peak temperature. Exceed it and they burn. Were that to happen a good part of the government of Britain ceases. Full stop. I do not enquire of the specifics.

These places are triumphs of engineering. But go to the peak achievements of previous eras, the Hoover Dam or the Elan Valley, and their visitor centres inform and educate. My admission here, simply to witness these racks an hour's train journey from London, has required a passport, a written record of my identity and a phone call to an upward superior for authorisation.

The site has every manner of safeguard built in. The generators here too are ready and primed for the failure of the electricity grid. A huge storeroom contains nothing but industrial-specification batteries for the collapse of the supply of oil. These data centres are not just the hubs for chat, shop and sexual witness. The food supply chain is tight with only a few days' stock in the pipeline. The wires go dead and Europe has three or four days of civil society. Then it is martial law and Britain becomes *Mad Max*.

These rows upon rows of racks have a life to them in the constant flash of the tiny LEDs. The data flows in and out are mediated by clusters of wires by the dozen. The what of their content is confidential but the physical stuff is open for explanation. The most common label is that of Cisco, a company name, like Oracle, little known to the average smartphone user. The box at the bottom is a firewall and in truth the technical explanation of what is happening in between is nine-tenths lost on me. The unceasing roar of the air conditioners is no assistance.

This digital world has dispensed with disks. They have a lumbering speed that cannot match the requirements. This is all about the performance of SANS, Storage Address Networks Measurement measured by terabyte, a byte followed by twelve zeros. This professional world is one of intelligently multi-honed tier-1 networks and AMS-IX NANOG DE-CIX specifications. The wires are made up of bundles of three-millimetre patch cables, two and a half thousand apiece with each one containing one hundred and twenty strands. The strands are a quarter of a millimetre in diameter when clad. A couple of years ago, a single strand was easily doing one hundred gigabytes a second.

The locations in Oregon and Sweden are greenfield sites. But some data centres are intermingled with history. In Newport, Tredegar House and Park are minutes away. The vast Telehouse in London is in the shadow of London's O2 Arena. It was where the fledgling provider Pipex first set up shop and within the city's docklands history. The streets are called Nutmeg Lane, Coriander Avenue and Rosemary Drive. The data centre in Switzerland has made new use of a military site. So too my location today is a place once critical in the era of Cold War confrontation. If the hardware is solid state so too is the location.

On this site, and not so long back, a then state-of-the-art box had dedicated lines of communication that linked Downing Street and the White House. The systems blink and the air conditioners roar in a structure built to withstand nuclear attack. The walls that protrude from the ground are all angled to attain the maximum deflection of atomic blast. The entry chamber itself has a wall of eighteen inches of concrete. The door of steel is massive, its hinges eight inches in height to hold its weight. The only flimsy element is the flooring. It is designed to be pulled up for cable replacement or renewal. If I am visitor to the heart of modernity, the place is also a key part, and a fascinating one, of the history that was the context for my first forty years of life.

Back on the surface it is a colourless February day, cool but not so cold as in the depths of the bunker. I am out, but a little detail of me is down there in a miniscule reduced simulacrum. My name in full runs to eighteen bytes with its two gaps included. My identifying numbers and letters account for another nine. Should I interact with government the enquiry will reach into one of those SANS. I may be eighty kilograms of organo-chemical material but without access to those few data bytes my practical life would be cast in severe difficulty if not chaos.

In her Tony Hill series, crime writer Val McDermid features a forensic computer scientist among her characters. Stacy Chen is with the good guys but she is not averse to using her talents against those she dislikes. At the close of *Splinter the Silence* a bad cop finds all trace of himself has evaporated from his bank's records. Eric Schmidt, Google Chair and a welcome visitor to 10 Downing Street, was a guest at the Hay Festival in 2013. A questioner declared he had no activity on the Internet and wanted to opt out. That is no longer an option, said Schmidt. "You're in, whether you want to be or not."

February 2016: Southern England

Wherever There Is Arbitrariness, There Is Also a Certain Regularity

The British Computer Society has a branch in west Wales and the branch has its meetings. But it has never had a meeting like this. The Chair announces that it has attracted the largest audience ever and a delay is likely. Another lecture theatre is being sought with all the apparatus of video link connection. In the event the organisers find that the unexpected throng of visitors in the departmental lobby can just about be packed, albeit closely, into the lecture theatre as advertised. The visiting speaker is Dr Mark Baldwin from Cleobury Mortimer. He is a formal figure in three-piece dark suit and yellow-blue striped tie. The reason for the crowd he has attracted is the object on the desk in front of him. It is an Enigma machine, the encrypter used by the German armed forces which was broken by the team of thousands at work at Bletchley Park.

Baldwin bubbles with enthusiasm for his subject. His knowledge and detail easily fill an hour's time-frame with an interest that never flags. The most immediate aspect of the machine on show is its solidity. Its coding was sophisticated, generating variations running into the hundreds of millions but its engineering belongs to the electro-mechanical era. Its materials are wood, brass and Bakelite. It comes in a wooden casing of solidity, fifteen inches deep and eight inches high. Its alphabet keys are circular of a diameter the size of an adult index finger. The instructions are headed by *"Zur Beachtung"*, printed in large lettering on a metal plate. The plate itself is fixed by rivets to the inside of the wooden lid. The electrical parts are housed within a protective casing of galvanised steel. The changeable plugs added an extra level of mathematical complexity. They are a solid two centimetres in length. The Enigma machines were not lightweight items of campaign equipment.

Baldwin's love and admiration for his machine are palpable. He is similar to one of the Bletchley Park team who admired it as being a thing of beauty. John Herivel looked at "the function of the wheels with their studs, pins, rings and serrated flanges, how they could be taken out of the scrambler." In its tactility he cherished "the wonderfully ingenious way each of the three wheels was forced into three of twenty-six equally spaced allowable positions where they were firmly held yet not so firmly that they could not be turned by finger pressure on the flanges to any one of the other twenty-five allowable positions." It was Herivel who detected that the fineness of German engineering was let down by fallibility on the part of its human operators. Even in the tapping of letters a human being cannot help but leave a signature trace.

Like all things of beauty it has its aspect of apparent simplicity. The keys, wires and pads of the main apparatus are supplemented by the extra layer of coding that the board to the rear provides. This addition of simple manual intervention produces variations of ten to the power of twenty zeros. By the time of its modification from the first version the number of Enigma's possible combinations came to exceed the number of atoms in the universe.

Engineering is one part of Baldwin's talk and the machine's history a fascinating other. The first machine was patented by its inventor, Arthur Scherbius, as early as 1918. A company, the *Chiffriermaschinen Aktiengesellschaft*, was established for its manufacture at Steglitzerstrasse number 2, Berlin. In an irony of history his first prospective customers, the Foreign Office and Navy of Germany, showed no interest. The inventor then made it available on the open market. Its availability allowed a trio of gifted mathematicians to break the code. Poland in the interwar period had a focussed eye on the re-arming of its neighbour. The Department of Mathematics at the University of Poznan broke the code of the first-generation machine and its work was shared with Britain. The British Government had itself bought one in 1926 but the War Office had decided it was too cumbersome for campaign use. The German Air Force came to differ from its fellow services. Its adoption of the technology removed it from the open market and the machines were manufactured by the thousand.

A Polish-French-British conference was held on 25–26 July 1939 at the Polish Cipher Bureau facility. Dilwyn Knox from Britain met the Polish mathematicians Jerzy Rozycki, Henryk Zygalski and Marian Rejewski, who shared their code-breaking work. Rejewski made the statement: "Wherever there is arbitrariness, there is also a certain regularity. There is no avoiding it." The encryption had its vulnerabilities. A letter could not be encrypted as itself, an exclusion that was an entry point. Repetitive weather reports or the greetings between German commanders were minute elements of predictability. The ears at Bletchley Park noticed a number of German radio operators were ignoring instructions. Machines were being started with the same settings each day. On April 20th 1940, the machines all across conquered Europe transmitted messages that were near identical. A great engineering culture was ever subservient to politics. April 20th was the Leader's birthday and its acknowledgement was mandatory.

Baldwin is a lecturer on the period but he is also a publisher. The wealth of literature on Bletchley Park is ever burgeoning. The reasons are several, the publicity of film and television being as much reflection as cause for interest. As it happens the machine before our eyes has appeared on film. Baldwin shows on screen his correspondence with a buyer for the film company that made *The Imitation Game*. He approves of the company's fidelity to authenticity that a real machine appear in the film. He is curt on other aspects of the makers' fidelity to history.

The film has given history a kicking. A tight budget may be behind its depiction that Ultra was dependent on a single Bombe machine. In truth there were two hundred at Bletchley Park. The most revealing aspect is how faithlessness to history criss-crosses with cultural cliché. Thus a boss in the services must mean upper-class and unpleasant in the translation to drama. The Commander Deniston as he lived was trilingual after being educated at Bonn and the Sorbonne. He was small and possessed of enormous patience. His son said that he was not "a man who found leadership easy. He lacked self-confidence. He was a highly intelligent self-made Scot who found it difficult to play a commanding role among the bureaucrats and politicians with whom he had to deal." To Aileen Clayton of the Women's Auxiliary Air Force he "seemed more like a professor than a naval officer." The real man is more interesting than the boss-toff made for filmdom.

The other aspect is the cliché of mathematics equals science equals boring. Turing is acted in a style of Aspergers-by-numbers when he was quite the opposite. It also strangely pushes him into a position of traitor. The plot imagines a confrontation with John Cairncross. The spy for the Soviet Union threatens exposure of Turing's sexuality and he goes quiet. It has an absurdity that military decisions are taken by a cluster of mathematicians. It is not even nice to women. Women by the thousand participated and are written out. At the end of 1944 the project had a staff of 8,743, of whom 75% were women. The work they did on the Bombe machines required intense concentration. They were issued with tweezers in case of wires touching. The plugs had to be inserted absolutely straight or they caused a short-circuit.

* * * *

The crowd that has so surprised the organisers of the British Computer Society is evidence of the fascination that Bletchley Park excites. The reasons are threefold. The historical line of engineering marches from Bletchley Park across seven decades to the server farms in the polar zones. But there is a nostalgia too. The company that manufactured the Bombe machines was a world leader. It went through various mergers and was finally acquired by a Japanese company in 2002. There is the central presence of Turing, a figure who should have ascended to Companion of Honour and more, and did not. It has an archetype story behind it of David versus Goliath and a moral straightforwardness of a manifestly good force pitted against a force that was manifestly not. It required a massive concentration of intellectual resource across the disciplines.

A last aspect for fascination is the secrecy that was sustained for so many decades after the end of the war. The reasons, suggests Mark Baldwin, were several and rooted in the culture. Deference to government was greater and the media had a sense of itself that was different. But it goes further. We can have no sense now of being within a militarised society engaged in total war. The Official Secrets Act had been passed in 1911 in the face of the perceived dangers from a belligerent Wilhelmine Germany. It had twice been strengthened and every recruit was presented with it. It was a vast document that required signature. One of the thousands of women remembered a Wing Commander who thrust it at her. "It clearly states that if, by doing any of the things I have warned you against, you disclose the slightest information which could be of use to the enemy you will be committing treason." His warning did not get any blunter and its substance was understood in all its literalness.

The physical geography of the huts was arranged to maintain secrecy. They were divided to house discrete activities and inter-hut discussion was forbidden. The "need to know" rule was universally applied. A messenger had a sister who worked in Hut 10. "I never knew what my sister did in Hut 10. I never even asked her. She wouldn't have told me anyway." The secrecy had teeth. "My memory of it" said a veteran "is never to talk to anyone about what you do, even to your fellow workers, and, if you do so, you may be shot."

This message of extreme punishment for breaching confidence runs through the memories of veterans. A briefing officer said that disclosure "would be liable to the extremest penalties of the law and I'm not sure whether, at the moment, that's hanging or shooting by firing squad." "You just assumed you'd be shot", said yet another participant. This generation is now that of our great-grandparents. They were members of another Britain, far different from popular memory and its balms of comfort.

February 2016: Aberystwyth

War: What Is it Good For?

The picture on the lecture theatre screen is of Dominique Strauss-Kahn. The occasion is his arrest in New York in 2011 on accusation of rape. The head of the IMF had to do the perp walk in cuffs. "That ended his chance of becoming France's President", says Ian Morris with a reflection, "this did not happen in classical Rome." The apposition of a twenty-first-century presidential aspirant and the house of Caesar is characteristic. Ian Morris is a historian who writes history across a big span. The jump from New York to imperial Rome is not even big by his standards. He is in London to talk about a book on different forms of hierarchy. Its span is twenty thousand years of human activity. Stone-age humans are a long way back but humanity's central activity is unchanged. It is the capture of energy from the environment for conversion and consumption via the human mouth.

The two thousand kilocalorie a day necessity in a time of foraging entailed loosely bound communities. Twenty thousand years ago the human population was half a million. Density of people was low and food resources were high. By the year 1800, the human population of the world had increased to four hundred and fifty million. The percentage who lived by forage was down to just 1%.

An agricultural society necessitated hierarchy. By six thousand years ago the societies of Mesopotamia and Egypt were capturing ten thousand kilocalories per person per day. That excess allowed for the building of Babylon and the Pyramids. By 1970 the industrialised economies had two hundred and thirty thousand kilocalories per person per day. One hundred billion tons of carbon have been converted since 1700.

Ian Morris is a visitor from California but his air of relaxation indicates he is on familiar territory. He is on a visiting Professorship. He illustrates the age of fossil fuel with a picture of a cluster of smoking factory chimneys. It comes, he says, from his home town in northern England. In figure he is immensely tall, resembling one of the small pool of actors always chosen by Hollywood for the role of diplomat or company chairman. His demeanour and tempo of speech are far away from establishment figures. He speaks with speed and enthusiasm. California would like him well. He handles questions deftly and modestly. He is queried on a specific point in the fine grain of history and admits that his study works better at the level of abstraction. Satisfying every nook and twist in history's turning is less easy.

A voice from the gallery asks how his taxonomy of power equates with Marx. Is conflict not inevitable across hierarchy's levels? The reference, says Morris, is like a reminder of an old and now little-mentioned acquaintance. He recalls the time when he was a postgraduate student. No-one then ever asked if you were a Marxist; the only question was what kind of Marxist.

Morris has in fact written about conflict, albeit its outward conduct rather than between levels within hierarchy. He has come to conclusions that are provocative and unsettling. Morris himself has not been in war although he was once a few hundred yards away from the attack of a suicide bomber. The results of his research have shocked him. "After all, war is mass murder. What sort of person says something good can come from that? War has made the world safer, which will probably raise a few eyebrows."

Dominic Sandbrook, a fellow historian, had an unusual opening to his review of *War: What Is it Good For?* "Even before I had opened this book, I wanted to hate it." The reason is that "according to Ian Morris war is not merely a necessary evil, it is actively good for us." Those calorie surfeits of the agrarian societies were not deployed only to build the Gate of Ishtar and the Great Pyramid of Cheops. They were used for the waging of organised warfare.

Morris roams across archaeology, anthropology and evolutionary biology in addition to military history. Humans live within ordered societies as a result of the restriction of violence which is the natural means to resolve conflict. In Europe, and many countries the world over, the state has been given a monopoly to use violence. Morris started as an archaeologist. The skeletons from ten thousand years ago regularly show evidence of injuries. Around one in five people met a violent end. The proportion is similar to that in studies of today's tribal societies.

For the armies of the agricultural societies the destruction of neighbouring territories made no sense. Power accrued by assimilating other peoples on productive territory. Larger units spurred innovation and industry. Rome expanded to a population of a million. The Roman Empire achieved a scale half the size of the continental United States and contained sixty million people. Two-thirds of its people, Greeks, Syrians, Jews, Egyptians, lived in complex urban societies. Twenty million outside, the Celts and the Germans, lived in rural, tribal societies.

The next cities, Antioch and Alexandra, were around half the size of Rome. Large markets and good transport accelerated economic specialisation. Ships grew bigger. Economies of scale bought reductions in transport costs. With the stamping out of low-level violence by 1250 one western European in a hundred was murdered. In 1550 it was one in three hundred. In the 1780s, the rate was one in a thousand. In 1950 death by murder was one in three thousand. States may not be a prerequisite for happiness or even justice but they are the bedrock of order.

Listening to Morris is to feel the great distances of time shrink. At Vindolanda, on Rome's imperial border in Northumbria, a cache of letters was uncovered dating back to year 90 of our era. Burial beneath a soaking of faeces and urine had inhibited the access of oxygen and ensured their survival. The topics differed little from front-line letters from twenty-first-century Afghanistan. The weather is lousy. Beer, decent food and fresh socks are all in short supply.

Morris compares the Boer War with Iraq. Both were pre-emptive attacks and the invading forces from the global power were the same size. But Britain lost twenty-two thousand in the first war and was murderous in return. One in thirty South Africans died at vastly greater cost. The Boer War cost one-third of British annual GDP at the time, Iraq around one-sixth of America's.

Morris' numbers are harsh. Europe reduced the population of the Americas by a half, the larger proportion by epidemic. But life outside the state had been hazardous. In 1385 in Crow Creek, in South Dakota, at least four hundred and thirty-eight people were slaughtered and thrown in a ditch. The violence was extreme with scalpings, beheadings, eyes removed and tongues excised. The archaeological evidence is consistent with the thesis that violence between groups is the first state of human interaction. The victims were indiscriminately men, women and children.

In 2012 globally one person in four thousand, three hundred and seventy-five died of violence. The latest forecast is a death rate of 0.7%. The gradual reduction has been from the Stone Age peak of ten to twenty percent. It is the paradox of the twentieth century. In 2010 the average human is four times as wealthy, four inches taller and lives twice as long as a great-grandparent of 1910.

Humanity perplexes. On the London lecture podium Morris speaks of fairness. A sense for the just is an intrinsic part of biological hard-wiring. That is the reason why he opened with his picture of Strauss-Kahn. It is historically revolutionary that a candidate for a Presidency be laid low by the accusation of a hotel maid. That is a historian's eye on placing the present in a context of the past. He is also a Californian resident, place of the planet's greatest assembly of technology brainpower. He turns to Ray Kurzweil, Google's Head of Engineering, for his information on super-computing and artificial intelligence. Not so far away in time a mind may be digitally replicable. "That means," says Morris with a tone of great cheer, "there will be two of you." One is a damp piece of degenerating chemical and organic material, the other an ever-fresh sliver of silicon memory. That, he muses, is just a start. Network them and the human mind becomes one vast cerebrum of inconceivable potential. This is Marvel Comics' Professor Xavier and his giant Cerebro made real. It is also the end of war. If humans are part of one being there can be no cause for division.

Scepticism is a wise part of the human make-up. Forty years is the adult span between last youth and first decrepitude. To be alive in 2016 is to be in a place inconceivable in 1976. 1976 was unimaginable in 1936, and so too in the opposite direction is 2046. Whatever 2046 is to be like, a young voice may still be lobbing his question as to how it all equates with a Marxist taxonomy of power.

March 2016: London

The Digital Superhighway

The Whitechapel Gallery is an island of art in an ocean of London in flux. New towers of glass loom to the west. A low building to the south dates from the eighteenth century and carries an inscription of its purpose. "The Proof House of the Gunmakers Company the City of London Established by Charter Anno Domino 1637." The entry to the Gallery itself has a wobble to its arch. The exterior is a masterwork of art nouveau. A plaque records that it was the home of Isaac Rosenberg, poet of the First World War. To the east down the High Street is the Blind Beggar pub where Ronnie Kray committed murder in 1966. None of the eye witnesses who were there were prepared to testify in court. Humans share killing with other species. Telling stories is an activity that humans alone do, and narrative is the subject on display at the gallery.

Three weeks after a close encounter with the Cloud it is occasion for the art of the electronic world. The exhibition's title is *Electronic Superhighway (2016-1966)* and its place in art's history is related at its start. This is art whose presentation comes packed with comment. The exhibition title itself dates from 1974. Korean video art pioneer Nam June Paik used it to foresee a globe connected by networks of technology. The exhibition itself is a retrospective over five decades of the relationship of artists with the Internet. It is stated in large and bold print but it is a loose premise in terms of scholarly precision. The fledgling ARPANET did not even carry its first data packets until 1969. Artists' awareness of its existence prior to the World Wide Web is not likely.

The great routes of information flow have always invited

excitement. When the first cable was laid across the Atlantic in 1858 it was celebrated with parades, poetry writing, one hundred gun salutes and church services. This exhibition locates itself, as part of a grounding, in a tradition. Large and frequent signage is everywhere. In 1968 the Institute of Contemporary Arts in London mounted *Cybernetic Serendipity*, the first exhibition on the connection between art and new technology. It was hugely popular with another connection in art that assisted. It was at the height of the pop-art era which rampaged across the borderline that had held between high art and low art.

Electronic Superhighway (2016-1966) recalls a half-century of artists' use of technology. The machines have changed completely and the walk over the extensive two floors is to enter a past now vanished. It is a rumbustious, various, idiosyncratic, questioning show but also strangely unnourishing. The machines that the makers have used are obsolete. That fact casts reflection on the meanings that they were intended to embody.

The first sight is a recent work by Olaf Breuning titled *Text Butt*. Giant buttocks of neon loom over the entrance door. The term "You're talking out of your arse" is made material and monumental. From one cheek emanate the words, "Did you had fun last night?", to which the other replies "Whaterver you think." The spelling is deliberate. Texting becomes art but it is art that is blunt and appears to offer just condemnation. But social media are simply bigger than disapproval. It has many aspects that ask for imaginative application. There is the blurring of private and public statement. Most users believe it to be private space akin to the randomness and spontaneity of conversation. Others advise that writers should think of it as a large billboard on a road side. If you are happy that it displays publicly what you intend to write, then go ahead. If not, do not. It is a misapprehension of privacy that has consequences. Suggest a meeting down town for purposes of a riot and it will send the author to court and quite possibly gaol.

Technology has repercussions across the spectrum of civic, commercial, economic and political life. The tech giants are public companies whereby insiders maintain privileged voting rights ahead of other shareholders. Europe and the USA divide regularly over basic concepts of privacy, market concentration and regulation. There are many issues but politics are absent in this exhibition. It is not that art should be a substitute for journalism but there is a prevailing sense of detachedness here.

A wall of bulky analogue TV monitors forms *Internet Dream* from 1994. They evoke a modest response of memory from older viewers. It is hard to imagine more than a yawn from young viewers who appear not to feature highly among the visitors anyhow. The graphics of yesterday are low in quality. A film, *Grosse Fatigue*, layers video clips, photographs and internet screen-grabs over one another as proliferating browser windows. As a metaphor maybe it is interesting. But there is a moral disquiet at the fringes of this world. Young people have taken their own lives over a bullying that has followed them from school to home and into the night. Vague playings by artists with electronics somehow seems not enough.

The most interesting is often the most historical. EAT, Experiments in Art and Technology, was an artistic collective led by Robert Rauschenberg and an engineer, Billy Klüver, who presided over happenings in 1960s New York. Their record is a flickering black-and-white film. Swedish artist Ulla Wiggen painted circuit boards and computer interiors with an echo of Mondrian geometry. Allan Kaprow, the inventor of the Happening, mounted an event called "*Hello*". Groups of artists and scientists in different locations communicated through banks of television screens with shouts of "I see you". Peter Sedgley, also in the 1960s, made glowing circles that change colour with the application of different lights shining on them. It is the show's guilty secret. Art gives pleasure through new shapes and new colours. It contrasts with the artist from Japan whose output is reminiscent of Malevich. But there is a difference. Malevich is rich in colour contrast and tonal variation so that his canvases contain volume. The electric printer does not do tonal variation so its output can do line but not depth.

Sedgley's work is about the eye of the recipient. It is for the viewer not the maker. As the works move towards the present day a kind of electronic narcissism grows. An artist puts his "blackness" up for sale on the web's online auction site. A self-defining art philosopher presents a vlog called *Art Thoughtz* which looks at art issuez of our timez. An artist takes his clothes off and prances for display in his own self-limited world. Traditional media of art are rare. Some paintings depict people posing in a chatroom. They have to be done quickly because there is no guarantee that the artist's subjects will stay for long. One subject masturbates. The results, if seen as entities in their own right, are disconnected from the Internet. It is up to the accompanying explanation, in print on the wall in the carbon-based world, to make the connection between art and the machine.

Large signs display credos for today. "Reality will soon cease to be the standard by which to judge the imperfect image", declares a standard-bearer with a room of his own. "Instead, the virtual image will become the standard by which to measure the imperfections of reality." In truth, this artist's room is not busy. At the exhibition of Picasso's portraits, six miles west of the Whitechapel Gallery, the rooms are full and the queues are substantial.

Technology has always invited comment in a mixture of anticipation and apprehension. In the *Phaedrus* Socrates was worried that the dialectical nature of knowledge would die out with text. Text was inert: ask it a question and it cannot respond. Technology has always provided the metaphors for the inner workings of self. For the thinkers of the Enlightenment, the mind was a mill that ground its contents into finer substances. The mind progressively became an electric circuit and latterly the brain is cast as a parallel processor. A new metaphor is given here by Hito Steyerl from *Too Much World: Is the Internet Dead?* dating from 2013. "The all-out Internet condition is not an interface but an environment ... living and dead material increasingly integrated with cloud performance, slowly turning the world into a multi-layered motherboard."

It is an intriguing metaphor. In one reading, the mainspring of time is a process of self-revealing on the part of the universe to a curious humanity. The universe possesses no knowledge of itself other than that recorded by us. But this is an art that does not go in for much cosmic speculation. The basic disparity is not here. We, the carbon middleware, have many deficiencies. Our memory is not reliable, our notions of logic or cause and effect are all over the place. But we can nip up the gallery stairs smartly. We can nip back out onto Whitechapel High Street faster than a machine. We can enjoy the change of colours. Most of all we can speculate about ourselves, even compose a response to three floors of screens and flashing LEDs. Whether artificial intelligence will ever deliver self-speculation, which is after all the root of moral action, is as unknown as any other part of the future. But this Superhighway does seem to miss the main road much of the time.

March 2016: London

Waiting for a Beaver

Gerald of Wales lived around the years of 1146-1223. In the record of his travels he had a sharp literary eye for what he saw. He termed the River Teifi noble with the finest salmon in Wales. At Canarch Mawr he watched the fish ascend the cataract, their biggest leap as high as the longest spear or like a bow let loose. Gerald liked everything he saw at the place, the church dedicated to St. Ludoc, the mill, the bridge; the orchard with its garden he called delightful. He was also admiring of the river's beavers. "I think it not a useless labour", he writes, "to insert a few remarks respecting the nature of these animals."

The natural world is perceived through the filter of anthropomorphism. A gift brought back from Dubai of chocolate made from the milk of camels feels different. It should not but does; its chocolate squares contain associations. Beavers appeal to us. They may focus their lives, like the rest of us, on eating, sex, snoring. But they are also, like us, builders. That makes them appealing; so too was their effect on Gerald of Wales. He respected "the manner in which they bring their materials from the woods to the water, and with what skill they connect them in the construction of their dwellings in the midst of rivers." His observations were close-up on the way that they moved wood. "Some of them, obeying the dictates of nature, receive on their bellies the logs of wood cut off by their associates, which they hold tight with their feet, and thus with transverse pieces placed in their mouths, are drawn along backwards, with their cargo, by other beavers, who fasten themselves with their teeth to the raft."

The building skills are formidable. "The beavers use such skill in the construction of their habitations, that not a drop of water can penetrate, or the force of storms shake them." There are beavers now at Blaeneinion Farm in the uplands beyond Machynlleth, whose homes are as described by Gerald. "They entwine the branches of willows with other wood, and different kinds of leaves, to the usual height of the water, and having made within-side a communication from floor to floor, they elevate a kind of stage, or scaffold, from which they may observe and watch the rising of the waters."

Gerald may not have known it, but beavers are vegetarian and monogamous. Rendered extinct across Europe they are being reintroduced in small measure to a background of contention. Gerald identified on the Teifi only one predator species. "Nor do they fear any violence but that of mankind." In his record of the hunting of beavers he goes far back to the time of Cicero and quotations from Juvenal. Beavers provided food and fur but the science of later centuries discovered one attribute that was unique to beavers.

The underfur is uniquely barbed, a quality that causes it to bind well when stewed in a mix of copper acetate and mercury-laced Arabic glue. Pounded and dried it made the very best felt for the best hats. This thatching quality of beaver fur made it superior by far to the next best substitute, the mixing of wool with rabbit fur. The hat-makers of Europe first trapped and killed the beavers in their own locality to extinction. The hunters moved on to the lesser populated regions. In Scandinavia too they were also made extinct. The opening of the Americas opened new areas of supply. The pioneer Samuel de Champlain was presented with fifty beaver pelts by the chiefs of the Hurons. It coincided with the explosive growth in wealth of the Netherlands. A new source of supply from Canada sent the price soaring. In 1610 the price of a beaver hat was ten times that of a wool hat. The ever-bigger brims and the luscious hats are a staple in the paintings of Vermeer.

The record of Britain's last beaver was that of the animal killed in Scotland in 1526. They survived in lesser numbers in France, Belarus, Germany, Mongolia, Norway, Russia and China. The population in Norway dropped to a hundred in 1880 but the predator species changed its habits and decided to let them return. By the 1930s Norway had seven thousand and they were reintroduced into Sweden and Finland.

Trial reintroductions were made in Britain. In Argyll beavers were released in Knapdale Forest in 2009. Unauthorised release has also taken place along the Tay and around one hundred and fifty are estimated now to be in the river and its tributaries. The Environment Secretary announced that beavers would be added to Scotland's list of protected species and "allowed to extend their range naturally." Their presence makes itself known speedily in their habitats. At a site in Devon they have built a lodge to live in and dug out canals through the adjoining land. Mud and sticks have built thirteen dams. In a matter of a few seasons they have turned the area of a woodland stream into wetland. A small zone is being returned to a condition of previous millennia when the beaver population ran into the millions.

The impact at the Devon location is cumulative. Inside the dams willow shoots grow, reinforcing the strength of the structures. The making of ponds encourages rushes, lilies, and sphagnum moss. That new shelter allows invertebrates under the surfaces. Frogspawn multiplies and kingfishers return. Humans who once had spear and gun now have solar panel and satellite. Rainfall data feed through to the University at Exeter where water volumes from the sky can be measured against its movement through the beaver zone. The beaver effect is clear. They dampen extremes, reducing peak water flow so it stays longer in the area.

In the Somerset levels to the north the call is for ever more concrete and canalisation. These small creatures are being revealed by science as nature's means to prevent floods. The reverse is also the case. Beavers also offset drought. The dams are not watertight. Water is slowed and stored but it flows. The filtration effects of the dams are also providing findings that surprise. The nitrates, ammonia and phosphorus of agricultural addition vanish in the mesh of willow branches, rush reeds, and mud. Less sediment and less toxic run-off in turn affect fish and estuary life downstream. The small species with the sharp teeth of orange colour is more than an animal; it is an entire ecosystem.

* * * *

I am in Burgweinting on a tiny tributary of the Danube. It is the country of Max Weber who coined the concept of the work ethic. He would have approved of the beaver. Burgweinting was once a separate village and is now a suburb three miles from the centre of Regensburg in Lower Bavaria. It has a line of old buildings along its ancient main road augmented by new developments. Northern Europe does its developments differently. The stand-alone house with its acreage of tarmac for multiple car parking is not the sacrosanct standard. Long curves of higher density terracing, three storeys plus basement, run alongside a shared piece of communal landscape. Five playgrounds are spread out over the distance of a kilometre. The area for strolling takes in woodland, river and marshland. This marsh area has been made a habitat for beavers and a sense of their presence is unavoidable.

Water sprawls in a directionless manner through the woodland. Dams are regular. Trees are gouged as a result of great gnawings. Gerald of Wales all those centuries ago described them as biting instruments. "The beaver has but four teeth, two above, and two below, which being broad and sharp, cut like a carpenter's axe as such he uses them."

This is a human-created landscape for the refreshment of urbanites. A series of signs writes about the animal inhabitants.

Beavers mate in the first months of the year. The youngsters, between one and five in a batch, have immediate swimming capabilities. They stay in the family home until the age of two. Their bodies are sculptured for swimming, their fur perfectly structured against wet and cold. The sign ends: *"Beobachtung ist möglich. Bitte ruhig behalten und Störungen vermeiden."* "Observation is possible. Keep quiet and avoid disturbances."

An April dusk is still cool and the dog-walkers and the family groups have gone home. The bridge over one of the many waterways is certainly quiet. The rumble of the motorway to Nuremburg is constant but distant. Patience rewards. After fifteen minutes the water ripples and a furry damp back glides under the bridge. There is a satisfaction to it. In part it is the uncertainty of the result and the patience that is asked for. In part it is the tiniest act of connectedness with an animal who commands admiration. It is a real-world experience between a member of one species and another.

Once achieved, another real-world experience is in order. Beyond the fringe of trees begins the zone of brick and concrete. It too comprises its complex system of devised water flows and release. Our water system has made clean a quartet of tankards. Weissbier flows amply to fill them. Our own group of four is also monogamous and we too are back in our warm habitat after a day's activity. Our own lodge and that of the beaver of my sighting are just three hundred metres distant.

April 2016: Burgweinting, Franconia

I'll Swap You Two Buggers for a Shit

The BBC. It has always been there. It is part of the national furniture. On my work trips in dull hotels a switch through the channels would find a slightly weird business channel with the BBC name on it. Citizens from other continents would laud the superior reliability of its news over their own government-assisted output. Its roadshows pop up in town squares and parks. In the Arts Hall in Lampeter its make-up experts came a few years ago to apply hideous scars and gashes to exuberant children. Its comedies and to a lesser extent its dramas are swathed in a moist nostalgia. The BBC has always been there and always will be. But perhaps not. So too was the Soviet Union. For seventy years it comprised a sixth of the Earth's land surface. Over a few months in 1991 it was gone.

Jean Seaton is the guest at Aberystwyth's Morlan Centre, the title of her talk *The Future of the BBC*. She is well suited for the task, being successor to Lord Asa Briggs as the Corporation's official historian. The season too is timely since the Secretary for Culture, Media and Sport has delivered himself of a White Paper just two weeks previously. Seaton has a clear view on the incumbent Minister and on former governments too. She repeats some base points. The notion that a broadcaster be independent of government has roots that go back nearly a century. Those roots are now so deep as to be unnoticed. She provides the historical grounding. The fledgling organisation had barely started before it faced a crisis. The General Strike of 1926 is unsurpassed as Britain's deepest social and industrial schism. The press, in private ownership, was hostile and its coverage partial. The nature of the news that came via the scratchy tones of a crystal radio set was different.

In truth Seaton's treatment of the payment system is slightly utopian. The direct payment of the licence fee is the bond that links every household to the Corporation. It is not payment to government and everyone feels their sense of ownership, at least in theory. Complaints against the BBC are rampant. Close scrutiny, however, of the mountain of moaning reveals that few call for the ending of the Corporation. The spread of BBC activity is large. Complainants universally want more of the bits that they like and less of the bits that they do not like. Mrs Thatcher, says Seaton, was not against a national broadcaster as such. She just wanted it to agree with her. But then no Prime Minister, it is said, in their heart really wants to be in Downing Street with just the *Daily Mail* for company.

Mrs Thatcher is important. Seaton's own book is the chapter of BBC history that covers the 1980s. Its title is *Pinkoes and Traitors*, a phrase borrowed from a spoof column in *Private Eye*. Her selection as author came about as a result of an unexpected visit by three men. She, said the trio, was their choice to continue the official chronicle of the Corporation.

Seaton is liberally inclined. That is with a large "L". She bows to John Stuart Mill. An argument is not for the winning or losing but for its betterment in the revealing of its issues. A Heideggerian sense of "Enthüllung" hovers. But Liberalism is under assault as much philosophically as politically. Human biology does not help. The limbic system is primed for rapid-fire decision as to friend or foe, response of smile versus fist. A philosophical strand has it that no knowledge is self-standing, no statement is free from partiality. Thus there can be no news coverage that is without self-interest. Impartiality may or may not be a chimera but an aspiration to it is noble. And it is bred into the Corporation, says its historian, in its culture, its instinct, its self-defence and not least its colossal rule-book. It is less the fact of impartiality that counts than its ever-constant pursuit.

Seaton's book covers the years 1974-1987 and to travel those years is to gaze into another Britain. There is for instance another side to that colossal book of rules. A distinguished Director-General, Sir Charles Curran, is quoted early in the book. "Good broadcasting is a practice not a prescription. In my view, traditions are more important in this respect than written documents, and I think that in this the BBC reflects the general character of British constitutional life. We depend more on the atmosphere in which we live than on the rules which come into existence as a result of the codification of that atmosphere." It is probably true. Corporate leaders do not read Kurt Gödel. No set of rules, runs his theory, can be both comprehensive and consistent. Curran has met the future Prime Minister early on. In 1969 he is invited to give a talk to the Finchley Council for Christians and Jews. "Curran", writes Seaton, "took the responsibility of educating Mrs Thatcher seriously."

The period was the worst for relations between politics and broadcaster. Her book is in part a tribute to the Corporation but also a picture of a media landscape from a far distant time. Part of the discord is down to the nature of the medium. Television eclipses radio and television wants pictures. The pictures of politics are dull. Women and men walk in and out of rooms and conference chambers, step off planes and out of cars. Peter Shore, a Labour front-bencher, chides the Corporation for its over-attention to certain rebellious MPs. They may be loud and shrill but they are not representative. But that is television's nature. It needs noise and tumult.

Organisational rearrangement is nothing new. Harold Wilson thinks relations between broadcaster and the Post Office are too matey by far. In 1969 he has it moved to the Home Office, a place, so he thinks, of greater rigour. Little changes. Labour has mooted bringing it into general government expenditure. Tony Benn, the hounder of young people's favourite radio stations in the North Sea, deems the Governors "undemocratic". Roy Mason, Secretary of State for Northern Ireland, in this telling threatens the BBC Governors with a permanent freezing of the licence fee unless it changes its reporting. In 1978 Labour plans to create three BBC management boards with half the membership appointed by the Home Office. Such a change never comes about due to the election of Mrs Thatcher. In a sign of the times the offices of the Director-General and Chairman are regularly swept for bugs.

Left and right continue in their conviction that the Corporation is secretly batting for the other side. The deviser of the cricket test for allegiance does not like the coverage of America's pre-emptive bombing raid on Libya. Norman Tebbit declares "the word 'conservative' is used by the BBC as a portmanteau word of abuse for anyone whose views differ from the insufferable, smug, sanctimonious, wet, pink orthodoxy". Six months on Tebbit produces a dossier to the effect that the coverage was "riddled with inaccuracy, innuendo and balance". BBC Drama of the era is a constant cause for outrage. One hundred and forty Conservative MPs demand that the BBC flush out the "Red Moles" who have infiltrated it.

In this period of industrial strife the BBC is as riven as the car industry. It pleases no-one. At the height of its difficulties *The Economist* attacks it for becoming a downmarket ratings-chaser. The *Evening Standard* accuses it of being run by unimaginative bureaucrats. *The Spectator* regards it as incorrigibly snobbish, anti-market and anti-British. The *Express* calls for its break-up. The age-old question burns as to whether culture makes behaviour or otherwise. Government voices believe that overly close coverage of the riots in Brixton is an encouragement to copy-cat behaviour.

As for the interminable internal problems, "to open any BBC

file from the seventies and eighties is to step into an alien and puzzling world." Seaton writes that "Machiavellian strategising about the Unions comes before anything else." The programme *Playschool* has a clock which for weeks does not work. It is the responsibility of an electrician to plug it in but its turning on is claimed to be the domain of another union. That is the responsibility of props workers who provide time cues. An entire Christmas Day narrowly escapes being blacked out. Live versus recorded music is constantly debated. Seaton does not mention this but once a hit started its descent down the charts it would be played in a cover version by session musicians. The cover was inferior and was a sure-fire prompt to send the teenage listener retuning for Radio Luxembourg.

A lamppost that appears on screen has different sets of attendants. The set is built by one group of employees, the post itself by scenery workers, the lamp by the props department. Palm trees made of Hessian are scenery but trees of glass fibre are props. The Corporation is trapped between official wage control policy from government and its position at the forefront of technology. The job description of a film sound recordist runs to twenty-seven pages. Craftsmen are on over-time but journalists are not. One and a half million pounds' worth of new computers are bought but their use is refused. New computers to cover referenda in Wales and Scotland are not even unpacked. A rigger punches his manager and his dismissal ends in a strike. The pay differential against commercial television soars to as much as 35% for some jobs.

At times charity prevails. The perennially popular *Crackerjack* has a live audience of children so that during a strike the whole show continues. It is simply not broadcast on television. These now look the strangest of times. History is made of small chances. Tess Swann, the wife of Sir Michael Swann, the Chairman, is a professional musician, a viola-player and prize-winning organist. A musical insider, she proves instrumental in the Chairman's intervention and a dispute being referred outside for arbitration. The Swanns are used to discord. At his previous role at Edinburgh University, relations with the student body had been fractious. A leading firebrand went by the name of Gordon Brown.

The past is a place of strangeness and its condemnation easy. The Cold War of the time was unabated. The number of missiles held by East and West peaked in 1986. The BBC was a very big beast and deeply implicated in the state. It had a role in planning for nuclear threat. It was directly involved in education from pre-school to the Open University. Half a million BBC computers were sold to schools. Its archives include the world's first collection of bird-song and its musical archive is the world's biggest. It was deep in the information war that was unbroken underlay of the Cold War.

"If television in the Western world uses its freedom", asks the Prime Minister in 1981, "continually to show all the worst that is in society, while the centrally controlled television of the Communist world and its dictatorships show only what is judged to be advantageous to them, how are the uncommitted to judge between us?" But culture is not just politics. The era pulses with innovation and the BBC is both custodian of culture and its maker. "I'll swap you two buggers for a shit" says the Head of Drama in a pub discussion with the director of *Brassneck* by Howard Brenton and David Hare.

A brief dip into the Cybersphere of today reveals that some aspects have changed and some not. "The BBC is the televised propaganda wing of the government", declares many a voice. That requires a true ostrich-in-the-sand view of its course through the decades. Class is to the fore. "TV Execs tend to be Oxbridge graduates who treat their audiences like colonial governors used to treat the 'natives' under their rule." As for those who direct it, "the BBC has been stuffed at the top with Tory placemen and placewomen since early on in Thatcher's reign. The BBC made a conscious decision in the early Eighties to stop making enlightening and meaningful drama about working class and poor people because it upset the Thatcher ideology."

The criticism veers to hyperbole. "It's now anathema to speak truth to power. Governments aren't there to be challenged, oppositions are. Ordinary people have melted away and their lives are no longer considered. Once *Panorama, World in Action* and others would report back social conditions in the UK. Journalists would question government." The BBC for these commentators was always better in the past. That is the nature of human memory.

Rage tends to characterise those who expend their energy in anonymous online insult-making. But it is illuminating how much love the era evokes. In truth Jean Seaton gives the impression of being a closer watcher of politics than actual programmes. News and current affairs count but there is no sense of bubbly response to the fun stuff or even the other programmes that manifestly hit the viewers and stayed with them for a long time. The rollcall of Alan Bleasdale, Alun Owen, Jim Allen and David Mercer are remembered as "superb and passionate writers" and the bloggers of today make contrast with the drama of Lord Fellowes of West Stafford.

The plays dominate the memories. *The Spongers, Spend, Spend, Spend, Edna the Inebriate Woman, The Firm* – Gary Oldman dispensing football violence rather than Tom Cruise in the Mafia's law outfit – *Made in Britain, the Boys from the Blackstuff, the Flipside of Dominic Hyde, Penda's Fen, Cathy Come Home, The Bar Mitzvah Boy, Scum* and *Licking Hitler*; these names occur and reoccur bathed in a warmth of memory.

Jean Seaton's book is the BBC's history. Her title at the Morlan Centre is the future. She summarises it in one line. Everything has changed except the arguments and they have remained the same. The function of the news is still to find the stories from the other side, to hold the ring. It is easier to say than carry out and selectively apply. Science deals in correlation and degrees of uncertainty. Unscience is aired on television because it is shrill and simple.

But Seaton on the future has a guide from the past. The prospects for radio were deemed dire not so long back. It would wither against the dominance of the image but technology intervened. A new mode of distribution demolished that particular item of futurology. The quality of signal improved and the car radio became universal. It speaks for all futurology. All futurology is wrong but we can never know how wrong. In print, newspaper production worldwide is at a historic high. It is only in Europe and the USA where print sales have plummeted. The e-book has its nice niche in certain genres but its share of overall book sales has flattened.

In one respect the situation of the BBC has not changed. For a generation, 1945-1967, its income grew on the back of a growing population. When Ken Russell filmed Elgar on a penny farthing on the ridge of the Malvern Hills money was in surfeit. A Board of Management report of the next era stated the problem: "It was poor but not that poor". Organisational culture runs deep. Penelope Fitzgerald, who won a Booker Prize, thought the BBC was "a cross between a civil service, a powerful moral force and an amateur theatrical society that wasn't too sure where next week's money was coming from."

The true unknowable is the next generation. The BBC's share-of-eyeball is going to drop. Ask a teenager about the BBC and they do not seem to know a lot. Mash-ups and parodies, music and home-made short-attention snippets are what they share. But then they know Radio 1. Ask around the older generation informally and enthusiasm for image rarely matches respect for radio. Share-of-eardrum could just as easily turn out to be the Corporation's secret weapon. The only certainty about the future is that it is not going to be the present extrapolated.

As for its survivability, an ultimate insider, Geraint Talfan Davies, characterised it slyly. "It is an organisation that is at once creative and bureaucratic, inspiring and infuriating. It manages to embrace the popular, the populist and the esoteric without any sense of discomfort, and is both wonderfully unworldly and cunningly political. It contemplates the world and its navel with equal enthusiasm, its core skills being programme-making and lobbying."

May 2016: Aberystwyth

An Elephant in Bremen

The best-selling postcard in the Ceredigion Museum is a picture of an elephant. The animal was a visitor to Aberystwyth and it is wallowing in the sea. Bremen on the North Sea also has an elephant but it is in the form of a monument. It is a strange and ungainly creation and is used by Richard Evans as an example of the elasticity of historical memory. Evans is a relaxed presence on a Hay stage. As a historian he is at the top. He is a knight, a Cambridge college President and author of an impossibly long string of books on the subject of Germany. He is one of a small number of historians who has a public profile beyond academia. In his treatment of counterfactuals – the writing of imaginary alternative histories – he has critiqued several of his eminent peers.

Evans has, he informs his audience, another distinction. It pops out by chance rather than through grandstanding that he is to appear in a major feature film. He was an expert witness in the celebrated David Irving libel trial of 2000. He is not appearing himself but is manifestly intrigued by the selection of actor who is to portray him. The theme of his appearance at the Hay Festival is Germany and memory. It is a testing topic for Germany.

Germany differs from other nations in not having a central place of power that goes back centuries. Berlin is an anomaly in having suffered two dictatorships. The DDR, the German Democratic Republic, poses some ambiguity. The camp at Buchenwald holds competing memories. One set of captives was released on liberation in 1945 but Buchenwald and other camps of Nazi rule were swiftly put to use again for a new class of prisoners. The site now has different memorials to different groups of victims.

Memory in Germany is concentrated in time. The era of one cataclysmic period dominates. The break-up of the Germany of the 1937 borders and the arrival of expellees by the millions in the new Bundesrepublik are etched deep in national memory. Awareness of the great expulsions is low elsewhere in Europe and sympathy for their victims non-existent. But it was the one determinant, says Evans, in the country's response to the implosion of Syria into war.

Germany differs too from its neighbours in the matter of its colonies. It was the first of the European powers to lose its colonies and for reasons that also differ. It had no Algeria or Kenya or Cyprus for the good reason that the end of the First World War brought the dispossession of its overseas territories. Evans is as good on this aspect of the history as he is on the later decades of descent into National Socialism.

The presence of imperial Germany in the Pacific region is scattered across the map in names that have been left behind. Bismarck himself had limited enthusiasm for the making of far-off colonies. "Not worth the bones of a single Pomeranian grenadier", he said. Nonetheless, the Bismarck Archipelago and the Bismarck Sea still survive. The colonies included Kaiser-Wilhelmsland, the Bismarck Archipelago, the now Solomon Islands, Marshall Islands and Caroline Islands. German New Guinea was founded in 1884 with Micronesia later incorporated into it. Bougainville Island and Nauru came four years later and Deutsch-Samoa in 1899.

They were lightly guarded. Samoa had a police force. On the outbreak of war a small gunboat, SMS *Geier*, and an unarmed survey ship, *Planet*, were assigned to what was called the "Australian Station". The *Geier* never reached Samoa and the island offered no opposition to invaders. On the morning of August 29th

1914 the island was invaded by soldiers of the New Zealand Expeditionary Force. Vice Admiral Count Maximilian von Spee of the German East Asia Squadron moved his cruisers SMS *Scharnhorst* and SMS *Gneisenau* to Samoa, arriving at the shore of Apia on September 14th 1914. However, he determined that a reinvasion would be unsustainable in a sea dominated by the Allies. The cruisers departed and left New Zealand in occupation.

Other islands were seized by the Australian Naval and Military Expeditionary Force. Japan too captured various German Empire colonies. On September 29th 1914, Japanese troops occupied the Enewetak Atoll, and on September 30th 1914 the Jaluit Atoll, administrative centre of the Marshall Islands. The Treaty of Versailles stripped Germany of its Pacific possessions and on December 17th 1920 the Council of the League of Nations approved the South Pacific Mandate. Japan took over all former German colonies in the Pacific Ocean located north of the Equator. This mandate included the Caroline and Marshall Islands. The cultural remains from this brief time of empire are slight but Samoa's leading poet is called Momoe von Reiche.

The expansion of Germany into Africa was more deliberate. In 1884 Bismarck declared that areas where Germany had economic interests of significance would become protectorates. The interests of the different zones of Africa were diverse. The lures in Togo and Cameroon were palm oil and rubber. In East Africa it was cotton and sisal. The vast spaces of South-west Africa attracted first cattle ranchers and then miners. This last territory was the site where the occupiers from Germany practised their most lethal assault, pre-echoing those to be carried out by the next generation.

Land seizures for the purpose of farming invited attacks in retribution from Africans. After one hundred and fifty settlers had been killed the home country sent fourteen thousand troops to support its colonists. The commander, General Lothar von Trotha, had a view of his task from prior experience. "My intimate knowledge of many central African tribes ... has everywhere convinced me of the necessity that the Negro does not respect treaties but only brute force." His method was physical separation between the races that was to be total and enforced by violence.

The principal tribe in the region were the Hereros. "Any Herero found inside the German frontier, with or without a gun or cattle, will be executed", ran the military decree. "I shall spare neither women nor children. I shall give the order to drive them away and fire on them. Such are my words to the Herero people." Men were killed and survivors, women and children, driven to the desert to starve. To his superiors he gave the justification: "I know that African tribes yield only to violence. To exercise this violence with crass terrorism and one with gruesomeness was and is my policy." The official publication of the General Staff in Berlin *Der Kampf* approved the campaign aim as "the extermination of the Herero nation".

The settlers and military in South-west Africa were joined by researchers. One was to become a leading "racial hygienist" for the regime of 1933. Hundreds of skulls were sent to Germany for study, the intention being to prove the dire results when the races were mixed. In 1907 the colony had banned intermarriage and all existing marriages between settlers and Africans were annulled. A new term was invented. "*Rassenschande*" means "race shame".

Another new word entered the language of German. Policy moved to the mass confinement of prisoners for purpose of labour. Its intended intensity was expressed in the new word of *Konzentrationslager*. The camps were of appalling rigour. On Shark Island off the coast rations were minimal, clothing was inadequate and the violence meted out for perceived work failures was extreme. Food in the camps was scarce. Prisoners had rice but no pots for its cooking. Horses and oxen that died in the camp were distributed for food. Dysentery was rampant. The routine of the day included the laying of bodies on the beach for their removal by the tides. Conditions in the camps were so set that death on a huge scale was inevitable. The purpose of extermination eclipsed that of useful labour. The Herero population was estimated to be eighty thousand at the war's beginning and was reduced to fifteen thousand over its course. The Nama tribe had an estimated twenty thousand and was reduced by half.

Opposition in the home country meant nothing. Protests from the Chancellor, Social Democrats and Catholic Centre Party were of no avail. The civilian governor in the colony was dismissed for calling the extermination "a grave mistake". A template for the future was laid down in the colonies. German citizenship was written as based on ethnicity rather than residence. The notion of racial differentiation against the neighbouring Slav countries of Europe became nascent. The first governor of South-west Africa was father to a more famous son, his name Hermann Goering.

Defeat in the First World War ended Germany in Africa and the victors divided their new acquisitions between themselves. In Germany the lost colonies were memorialised. Behind the railway station in Bremen an elephant in brick was raised to a height of ten metres. Terracotta tiles set in the plinth listed the lost overseas possessions. The speeches at its inauguration on July 6th 1932 praised the achievement of the colonies and demanded their restoration.

In 1985 the Whitaker Report for the United Nations classified the massacres as an attempt to exterminate the Herero and Nama peoples. It was deemed one of the first cases of genocide in the twentieth century. In July 2015 the German government and the speaker of the Bundestag officially called the events a "genocide" and "part of a race war". The elephant had survived the Second World War and remained in Bremen. Namibia became an international issue during its occupation by neighbouring South Africa. In 1990 the elephant was officially declared to be "an anti-colonial monument". In 1996 the first president of an independent

Namibia, Sam Nujoma, made a state visit to Germany. His itinerary included Bremen where a new plaque was unveiled. It read "In Memory of the Victims of the German Colonial Rule 1884-1914." Art is ever-elastic. The purpose of the monument from that day of inauguration was wholly turned on its head.

May 2016: Hay-on-Wye

The Hate Horrifies Me

The whole world comes to Hay-on-Wye. The first sight on approaching the entrance to the site of its literary festival is the great bulk of a sculpted head in the Toltec style. Hay has spawned festivals in India and Latin America. Hay goes to the world and the world in return comes to Hay. Nobel prize-winners are a regular. The Nobel laureate for this year comes from a country of our own continent that is little known. Belarus, if anything, is the byword for a state barely changed since 1989.

The vast other Europe, beyond the rivers Vistula and Dnieper, has featured regularly on the platforms of Hay. The Festival Archive contains a feature by Garry Kasparov titled *The Hay Lecture: Putin's Russia*. The lecture was delivered on May 31st 2008, lasts just short of an hour and is potent polemic. In it, Kasparov likens his country to a vast Potemkin village put up for display to deceive the visitor. Russia is better understood as a feudal state or more akin to the old *caudillo* republics of Latin America than a country of Europe. The inner circle pays tribute upward and they in turn extract their toll from their own circles of vassals. It is the economics of Tony Soprano. The President wears in public a watch that costs $160,000. He is, according to investigative journalism, quite likely the world's richest man. In one respect Kasparov's analysis has dated. The foreign affairs adventurism is less connected with a return to the USSR than maintaining a permanent sense of instability.

Hay in 2014 hosted a panel discussion: "Russia, Ukraine and Us". Anne Applebaum remembered that Russia for a time after the end of the Cold War was seen as a country in transition. Its journey was towards becoming part of the collective European polity. It was exemplified in membership of the G8 Group and the toying even with NATO membership. That period, said Ms Applebaum, is gone. Russia in its present form is a country on its own.

The journalist Oliver Bullough was also on the panel. Bullough lived in Russia for seven years and used his time to travel the vast country widely. His journeys far outside Moscow paint a picture of a country in the twenty-first century unlike any other. In particular he has been witness to the effect of the withdrawal of subsidy from the era of the command economy. The country's vast north is particularly affected. The Soviet Union had one hundred and fifty thousand villages in 1989. Since then twenty thousand have been abandoned and a further thirty-five thousand have fewer than ten inhabitants. With life expectancy lower than many African countries, the population is in freefall. The drop over 1989-2005 was twelve million. With the number of twenty year olds shrinking so sharply the UN is forecasting by mid-century a drop of thirty-two million. The population imbalance has geopolitical consequences. China's bustling Heilongjian region has a population of thirty-three million. It is geographically adjacent to a region in Russia of the same size but one-eleventh the number of inhabitants.

The economic fundamentals are well-known but repeated. The voucher privatisation programme of the early 1990s saw company managers and party members acquiring control of former state enterprises. Gazprom controlled a third of the world's gas reserves and a majority stake was sold for $230 million. The entire national electricity grid was sold for $630 million. The sectors were endless: cars, ports, ships, iron, steel, aluminium, airlines, banks, the world's largest diamond mines. Often cash was not even needed. In 1994–96 the state privatised one hundred and fifty state-owned companies for $12 billion. Most of the purchase was via a loans-for-shares programme for connected buyers from state banks.

Oliver Bullough digs beneath the surface and writes about drink and its long history. Prior to 1917, alcohol duty made up 40% of government revenue. The Leninist state was high-minded enough to live without it. The attempt was short-lived and ruinous. By 1940 Russia had more shops selling alcohol than fruit, vegetables and meat combined. Over the decades 1940-1980 consumption increased eightfold. Officialdom tried to disguise it. In 1965 the official statistics reported deaths from "external causes". Alcoholism was put in a category that encompassed murder, suicide, road accidents, poisonings and drownings. The deaths that year numbered 119,170, tripling by 1995. Four-fifths of car deaths were alcohol-related. Cardio-vascular deaths tripled. In 1975 alcohol was damaging one in eight rural children in utero. It was strongly implicated in STD transmission. The official response was to re-categorise alcohol sales. It was included alongside ice cream, coffee, cocoa and spices.

The panel discussion "Russia, Ukraine and Us" was chaired by Bridget Kendall. She is in Hay again in conversation with Svetlana Alexeivitch, the winner in 2015 of the Nobel Prize for Literature. As with the four previous winners from Russia the country has not been pleased. *Literaturnaya Gazeta* declared: "Alexeivitch is a classic anti-Soviet ... a traitor". The last is interesting as her father is Belarusian, her mother Ukrainian. *Izvestiya* has been plainer. "Not a writer", declares their critic.

The Nobel Prize Committee has shown flexibility in its choice. Literature need not necessarily mean fiction. Alexeivitch is a journalist but Kendall, an astute and acute presenter, describes the documentary writing as more harrowing than the tailored fashioning of fiction. She speaks through an interpreter of equal high skill. Alexeivitch speaks in her language whose rhythm is different from that of English. The sentences give the impression that they are being put together with difficulty. With time she relaxes and includes items of a grim humour. She met the newspaper reader who remembered the days of *Pravda:* "I buy three newspapers and each one of them has its own version of the truth. Where's the real truth?"

As a writer she is motivated by a purpose. "I'm piecing together the history of domestic, interior socialism. Socialism as it existed in a person's soul." The sweep of public policy in her writing is only featured where it has an impact on the lives of individuals. "I've always been drawn to the miniature expanse of the individual. It's where everything really happens." As for the voices she has caught: "I sought out people who have been so deeply penetrated by the Soviet idea that the state has become their entire cosmos, blocking out everything else, even their own lives. Such people couldn't walk away from history, dissolving into their private existence, allowing what had been minor details to become their big picture."

Her subject is Empire and its memory. For those born in or after the USSR: "it's like they're from different planets." She herself was just there at the right time. "I came into writing when this multi-nation empire was collapsing. I was just the right person in the right place. I met people who had met Lenin." The essence of her writing is the stance of witness. "A human is so complex that a pure chemical evil is impossible to find." But it is an openness not mirrored in a country with a military outlook of being surrounded by enemies and in a state of siege.

The dichotomy is stark. "Those who are not with us are traitors." But the past is treacherous. During Lent of 1918, Nicholas II in captivity blamed Jews for his fate and read aloud to his wife and children *The Protocols of the Elders of Zion.* In 1917 the Ipatiev House, where eleven royals were killed, was demolished by the order of Boris Yeltsin, the then local Party chief. In July 1998 the royal remains were reburied in St Petersburg's Peter and Paul Cathedral. In 2000 the family was canonised.

Kendall asks about the form that she has adopted. "I was raised in a village," says Alexeivitch. "Life is verbal, discussion is constant."

Kendall repeats the adjective applied to the work of "polyphonic". In its quality of polyphony Kendall asks who were the executioners and who the victims. "They were the same people," says Alexievitch. "A writer writes," she says, "but a writer also listens." A writer also speaks at a public event and every word that is spoken at Hay is gateway to those in print. The hour-long session is satisfying. The words and the incidents are contained in the book *Second-hand Time*. The Nobel laureate in person in Hay leads to the reading of the book. *Second-hand Time* is a monument.

* * * *

Alexeivitch has a clear purpose in her seven hundred pages. "I decided my story would be domestic socialism, how it was lived day in, day out. I would be a historian of overlooked feelings, the sort that big history ignores." She asks a woman who denounced her own brother in the purges, "What do you remember of 1937?" "I was in love", is the response, "and was loved." The accumulating power of the writing is that it holds back from judgement. A human is a part of a social whole and it is a military country with a military outlook which is surrounded by enemies. Her subject is a country that has no collective way of interpreting the experience of the twentieth century that made it. She observes the "absolute lack of desire to reflect on the main thing, Stalin and the war."

In Perm in Siberia a camp has been made into a museum. For the present day the staff have all been replaced and the emphasis realigned to be about those who worked there. The Soviet Union withered so suddenly that the disjunction between those who knew it and those who did not is abrupt. In the new order everything is for sale. A "For Valour" medal costs twenty dollars. The price of an "Order of Lenin" is a hundred dollars. A veteran protests to a policeman about the selling of military memorabilia on the street. The policeman shrugs: "These are relics of the totalitarian era."

The past is half-erased and part-continuity. The gargantuan statue of Felix Dzerzhinsky, the creator of the secret police, that was in Lubyanka Square was felled. Many other statues to him remain across the former Soviet Union. The Lubyanka itself is the prison and interrogation centre that haunts the memoirs and the books about the era. It now houses the directorate of the Federal Security Bureau of the Russian Federation, the FSB.

Alexeivitch remembers one of the giant projects of Stalinism. The White Sea Canal sought to join the White Sea to the Baltic. Between 1931-33 one hundred and twenty-six thousand prisoners worked on it, of whom a fifth died. Solzhenitsyn went to visit it decades on and saw it in a state of desertion. It had been built of an insufficient depth for sea-going vessels. One of Alexeivitch's voices speaks of the world that provided its labour force. "My grandmother was born in 1922. Her whole life people had been shot and executed. Arrested. That was all she'd ever known."

The memories are there just beneath the surface. The communal apartment had twenty-seven inhabitants sharing a kitchen and a bathroom. A prisoner remembers the water thrown over the captives who had failed to meet the required work norms. In a temperature of minus 40 these human ice statues dotted the landscape until Spring. The status of gaoler and victim had a randomness to it. Oversleeping and arriving ten minutes late for work was sabotage and earned a prison sentence. It eased with the end of the regime. "After '53 they stopped punishing lateness like that. After Stalin died, people started smiling again; before that, they lived carefully. Without smiles."

Alexeivitch joins a group at a beer-stand. The only subject is the country and its state. "People in the West seem naïve to us because they don't suffer like we do, they have a remedy for every little pimple", says a professor. "We're the ones who went to the camps, who piled up the corpses during the war, who dug through the nuclear waste in Chernobyl with our bare hands. We sit atop the ruins of socialism like it's the aftermath of war. We're run down and defeated. Our language is the language of suffering." But as for the next generation: "I tried to talk about this with my students. They laughed in my face: 'We don't want to suffer. That's not what our lives are about.'"

Alexeivitch was in Moscow on the tenth anniversary of the attempted coup of August 19th 1991. If it had succeeded, says her interviewee, "they would have saved a great country from ruin. Gorbachev and Yeltsin would have been put on trial for betraying the Motherland. They wouldn't have betrayed socialism. Russia needs a strong hand. An iron hand. An overseer with a stick." The overseer lives on in the writer's own country. A twenty-one-year-old was one of tens of thousands who gathered in October Square in Minsk in 2015. The riot police attacked and arrested hundreds. Fully armed soldiers were in the forests outside the city in readiness as a back-up force. To demonstrate, according to the law of Belarus, is an attempt to overthrow the government and carries a sentence of four to fifteen years.

Moscow is a city of Europe whose centre has come to resemble others. It is also a city of migrants. Tajiks in industrial accidents receive no treatment in hospital. The breaking of contracts and the stealing of wages are common. Riot police assault and kill immigrants with immunity. A mother receives the body of her son; the corpse has been stripped of its internal organs for sale. Theft in the army is widespread with conscripts brutalised and left under-fed. New soldiers are addressed as "fresh meat", "serf" or "worm". The infirmary has no medicines other than antiseptic after the beatings and the enforced eating of faeces. "When I look around Russia," says Alexeivitch, "the hate horrifies me, the necessity to hate someone."

Her subject is the life lived away from the centre and the heights. "No-one asks the small people. They are the disposables in this game." She visits a village shop in the Smolensk region. "You want to know about freedom? Have a look around our shop. There's vodka, any kind you like: Standard, Gorbachev, Putinka: heaps of cold cuts and cheese and fish. We even have bananas." This is a twentieth-first-century country in the northern hemisphere where a banana is cause for gratitude.

She comes across a survivor who has passed from Soviet Union to the new Russia. It is her last page of seven hundred. "What have I really lost? I've always lived in the same little house without any amenities, no running water, no plumbing, no gas, and I still do today. My whole life, I've done honest work. My whole life, I've done honest work. I toiled and toiled, got used to back-breaking labour. And only earned kopeks. All I had to eat was macaroni and potatoes, and that's all I eat today."

May 2016: Hay-on-Wye

Who Needs Empathy?
Automating the Professionals

The Susskinds awe to the point of being alarming. Father and son, they occupy a territory that joins Oxbridge college to Whitehall and Downing Street itself. That role where scholar blends into policy wonk has a price of admission: intellectual firepower and industry, confidence and brio are all part of it. The Susskinds, Richard and Daniel, are joint authors of a book on the impact of computing on work. It has received a high level of attention in the press. The human subjects of their book are the women and men who still buy and read the broadsheets.

The full title of this Hay-on-Wye event is *The Future of the Professions: How Technology Will Transform the Work of Human Experts*. Father and son are scarily intelligent but they also project an enjoyment in each other's company on a public platform. On the question of a book that has been jointly written the answer comes: "What can I say about my co-author? He has become like a father to me." The line may have been rehearsed, but it is good. A Hay audience, like any audience, responds to warmth.

The festival programme is succinct in its description of the event. "In a digital society we will neither need nor want doctors, teachers, accountants, architects, the clergy, consultants, lawyers, and many others, to work as they did in the twentieth century." The words that accompany this are not those of dry futurology. "Our current professions are antiquated, opaque and no longer affordable, and the expertise of the best is enjoyed by only a few." That last phrase is over-stated. Theology is freely available if sought from an army of vicars. Many of the fruits of great public architecture are open to all. The view to amaze from the tenth floor of Tate Modern's Switch House asks for, but does not oblige, a payment of £4. Zaha Hadid's stirring Aquatics Centre on the 2012 Olympics site has an entry price of £1. Nonetheless, something of consequence is afoot and the Susskinds are the first to fold it into an accessible whole and bring it to a wide audience.

They are alarming in their cerebral combination but differ slightly in personality. Father is extrovert on a public platform. Another book has been published this season. Its prose is jauntier as reflected in its title: *Only Humans Need Apply*. It is a guide to areas of work where the carbon middleware, the entities who fill a festival marquee, will have an advantage over silicon and cable. There is a nice quip that a work set-up in the future will comprise a machine, a dog and a human. The role of the human is to feed the dog. The role of the dog is to bite the human in the event of any idea of interfering with the machine.

The Susskinds run through some of the basics that underlie technology and its acceleration. Moore's Law starts and leads to Big Blue's mastery at chess. The triumph in the much more complex game of Go has been a breakthrough of astonishment at the heightened prowess achieved by the artificial mind. The generation of automated code is already common.

Richard Susskind's professional area is the application of information technology to the legal profession. He has been adviser to the Lord Chief Justice of England and Wales. He holds a professorship at University College London so the epicentre of Britain's law-making is a short walk away. The processes of transformation move in all directions. Online dispute resolution, virtual courts and the automated preparation of legal documents are all underway. The prediction is that a three-way change will cut a swathe through traditional practice. Deregulation, the disaggregation of legal tasks and the embedding of legal compliance within systems are a potent mix. Gabriel Zucman, the economist of taxation, has written that a global asset register is quite feasible. That realisation would mean a lot of redundant tax lawyers.

The elder Susskind's province is the law but the two turn their spotlight on education and health. They are not the first. One writer, Eric Topol, calls his book *The Patient Will See You Now: The Future of Medicine is in Your Hands*. They are beneficent in their thinking. The loss to the practitioners of professional expertise is to the gain of their users. Expertise will be more accessible, faster and hugely cheaper for its consumers. They draw analogy to the experience curve which drove the era of manufacturing. The radical drop in unit cost will enhance demand. The benefits for citizenship, personal health and education are great.

There is another side they do not address. Tom Cruise in the film of *The Firm* faces the mafia and tells them they are as much entitled to lawyer-client confidentiality as anyone else. He is not going to snitch because he is a professional. Walter White in the second season of *Breaking Bad* is detained in hospital after his kidnapping by his psychopathic crystal meth distributor. He has faked a period of total amnesia to cover his absence. Bryan Cranston narrows his eyes and quizzes his doctor as to how far goes his duty of confidentiality. It is total, runs the medical response. If you told me that you had an intention to kill someone, the doctor adds as an amendment, my ethics would require me to inform that person. It is not just that the machines never forget. Their liking for sharing is as great as their tendency to leak.

The old-age issue of "Who guards the guardians?" is not present. One of the regular computing fiascos of the public sector was the overweening project for the National Health Service. Its ethos was a result of the ill-discipline of government conducted from a sofa. Confidentiality was intended to co-exist with access from one hundred thousand data points. Low-cost access to professional wisdom may blur the demarcation between provider and customer. In the zone of Big Tech if you are not paying for the product then it is you who are the product.

William Caxton killed the profession of scribe. The typing pool of my first serious workplace was a paradigm for efficiency and is no more. New modes will make new work for para-professionals, process analysts and system engineers. The Susskinds forecast specialist empathisers. These already exist. Where clergy are no longer called to preside over funerals a new class of impressive lay professional has emerged as replacement. The Susskinds are buoyant but then they are among nature's survivors. The present will always reward those with the apparent gifts even to stab at a prediction of the future.

There are cognitive objections to this model. Knowledge is not just declarative and procedural. The management consultants, architects and barristers who are at the top of their game are there because they have reservoirs of reference that are implicit. That quality goes back to decades of experience of a physical world. The architecture of Zaha Hadid goes back to an absorption in constructivist art. A camera sensor is not going to perceive a Malevich canvas in the manner of the rods and cones of a biological eye.

The Susskinds do address this, wondering whether what they call gut reactions and intuitions of professionals are susceptible to formal articulation. They are tempted by the notion that professionals are reluctant to share this knowledge. It is not too convincing. Experts do not actually know how much they know, or rather it only becomes explicit when it is called upon to act. It is the Heidegger analogy of the hammer. Its true quality is only called upon when it is brought into action to perform its function. But the new profession of knowledge engineering may well integrate tacit knowledge into procedural algorithm.

Machines are doing well in one area where professional status is contested. "Counsellor" and "psychotherapist" are not protected titles although there are accredited registers such as the British Association for Counselling and Psychotherapy. Text-based counselling has taken off. *Babylon* has one hundred and fifty thousand users, *PlusGuidance* ten thousand, *BetterHelp* one hundred and fifty thousand registered users in Britain and *Talkspace* claims half a million users. There is an ethical issue. "If the person is in distress, there's a lot of anxiety for the practitioner because you can't see them", says a practitioner. But there is the intrinsic nature of the relationship with the screen. Its appearance of privacy induces the disinhibition effect. Issues are revealed faster and with more openness.

A central issue in the Susskinds' thesis is philosophical. It goes back to Plato. The question is as to how a society chooses to share its expertise. They find analogy in the protected status of the professions to the guilds of the middle ages. Much is already up and running. Online religious communities like *Beliefnet* and *Patheos* have memberships running to five or six million. *Cybersettle* and *Resolver* are used for dispute settlement. The trends are accelerating with the convergence of big data, artificial intelligence, speech recognition, neural networks and robotics. Affective computing is the computation of emotion. In this approach empathy is a cognitive activity which makes its simulation achievable.

There are voices to the contrary. The biggest and smartest consultancy in the world suggests that over the next forty years half of all work worldwide is ripe for automation. The report threatens wages that currently pay out an aggregated fourteen and a half trillion dollars. But then the OECD has come to a different conclusion. Only nine percent of jobs are vulnerable enough to be classified as high risk. This sounds high, but it is a norm for past industrial history. The report's methodology has been different.

Rather than looking at broad occupations it has broken work into components and tasks. That uncovers a high presence of activities that computers do not do so well. Creativity, social interaction, group work, person to person communication run across a wide spectrum of jobs or form part of their content. Book-keeping meets all the criteria for automation. It emerges that three quarters of its present doers cannot do the job without contact and collaboration.

The questions from the floor are varied. A parent says that her children are all sent to after-school coding classes. This is a very Hay Festival event. The Susskinds have different responses. One says why not. The other advises not to bother. Whatever the play-deprived infants acquire will be long redundant by the time they are adults.

"I'm an actor", asks a questioner, "should I be worried?" A philosophical turn of question asks if it will reduce empathy. The first evidence is tentatively suggesting that social media for some is reducing social skill. But cause and effect are unknown. The less socially adept may be the group most inclined to high usage. The Susskinds from the tenor of their responses have a brimful of empathy. But the response is, "Why are we so concerned about empathy? A lot of professional work is outcome-centred." It is true. But with that confirmation of a suspected cancer diagnosis it requires a different kind of human being to run through treatment options. Is a digital assistant really going to fill the gap?

The Susskinds do not mention one aspect of the glue that connects. It is not empathy. Empathy is probably secondary to another abstract and that is trust. Trust is much more than a nice-to-have aspect of going about our daily lives. Societies that are low in trust expend enormous resources on who may or may not be counted on. Trust is highest within some of the world's wealthiest countries. High trust and economic growth are closely linked. The retreat from trust in society results in the sole reliance on family and group. The blockchain has revolutionary possibilities. The Platform has had some great success. The buyer-seller reporting raises trust. In Lagos a ride-hailing Platform has aided security. The driver with a high rating is not going to be a kidnapper or extortionist.

But trust-building is slow and gradual and its demolition is rapid and abrupt. The social media giants do not score high on trust. The first cyber-doctor that kills, the first auto-solicitor that misses something out of the ordinary, a flying freehold for instance, and the game is up. The universe is not an algorithm. Kurt Gödel's theorem of 1931 still rules. No set of rules can be both simultaneously comprehensive and consistent.

June 2016: Hay-on-Wye

I Long the Arrival of the Ship with the Seeds

In the 1980s, when Neil Kinnock led the Labour Party, a weighty book was handed out to the shadow cabinet for its collective holiday reading. Its author, Michael Porter, anatomised the strategies for industrial competitiveness that favoured different countries. Britain, a lead country of the post-Empire group, was depicted as best suited for living off dividends, auctioning fine art and manufacturing breakfast cereal. The auctioneers are now American and French and the best-known cereal name has been acquired by a company from China.

But, of course, it is not easy for politicians. Britain's ninth-largest company spans the globe and is in an industry sector that did not even exist in 1980. When Labour came to power a decade on, its early Blair Cabinet members were also handed reading for their holiday time. The theme of one book was the psychology of happiness as discerned by a scholar in Chicago with the proper tools of research. Mikhail Czikszentmihalyi reported that across all the options for using leisure time, it was the activity of gardening that induced the most happiness in its practitioners.

The contents of the gardens of Britain are far removed from natural flora. They have become as they are due to a blend of science, trade and entrepreneurialism. On this June evening high humidity and a twenty-two-degree heat have created a crackle of lightning on the cliff journey north. The run of buildings that make Aberystwyth's Institute of Biological, Environmental and Rural Studies appears deserted but there is one place of life. In the furthest lecture theatre the Cardiganshire Horticultural Society and the Ceredigion Historic Gardens Trust are jointly hosting a summer guest lecture.

Andrea Wulf has the polish and finish of the public speaker used to regular practice. She is fresh from a thirty-venue publicity tour of the USA. Her subject there has been her acclaimed biography of Alexander von Humboldt. The book was three and a half years in the making and her travel in the footsteps of Germany's great polymath was formidable. The subject for this Monday night is a previous book that she has written. Its subject is closer to the audience than Humboldt. "The Brother Gardeners" are the chain of men who together formed the British garden as we know it.

No talk now comes without a screen, but Andrea Wulf uses it sparely. Her images are a means to illustrate rather than as a focal point to which words are subordinate. It is an uncommon speaker who can evoke a sense of how it may have been in a time that is not our own. Wulf does just that in her capturing the sheer thrill that the new discoveries created in her men and women of the eighteenth century. Their world brought excitement and colour to Britain.

The flora of the Americas were tightly packed into boxes by the hundred. Their crossing of the Atlantic made Britain the gardening fulcrum of the world. A country whose winter shades were uniformly brown became host to the reds and oranges of maple. Britain was once home to only four indigenous types of evergreen. Its naturalists were rapturous about the arrival of Scots pines at their country's ports. Today the gardening enthusiasts of North America come on pilgrimage to the gardens of Britain. These visitors, says Wulf, little know how much the sights before their eyes are indebted to the venturers and the merchants of the eighteenth century.

The brother gardeners of her talk are a group of men who

brought gardening to Britain. They were active in trade, science, discovery and exploration. Andrea Wulf's tale entwines these interlocking activities with fine art.

* * * *

Knowledge commences with the making of categories. Philip Miller (1691-1771) was a revolutionary force who for most of his working life managed Chelsea's Physic Garden. He transformed its lacklustre state. Quasi-medical in status it had originally supplied herbs to apothecaries and other practitioners. Under Miller its scope was enlarged to become, along with Kew Gardens, a repository of botanical knowledge. Miller divined the agency of insects in pollination. He wrote his life's work down in his *Gardeners Dictionary*.

The dictionary was hugely popular and influential. It advised on how to protect against frost and pests. It pointed out which areas of shade or direction favoured which plants. It showed how to make stoves, hotbeds and a thermometer. Alexander Pope declared the book was the one from which "you draw all your knowledge". There had been treatises before on gardening in small editions that were seen by the aristocracy, but Miller's work was new and compendious. The Prince of Wales himself was the most aristocratic horticulturalist of all. When the Duchess of Queensbury came to court she came in a sensational dress of white satin decorated with nasturtiums, honeysuckle and ivy. The time was right for guidance of authority. The dictionary not only propelled Miller into becoming an international authority on flowers but it jumped the class divide in its readership. It made Britain into a nation of gardeners.

In the era before science plant life was interwoven with myth. If a child picked motherdee, red campion, it meant death to the parents. If a woman in pregnancy stepped over cyclamen it meant miscarriage. The Doctrine of Signatures matched appearance in nature to medical application. The walnut resembled the human brain so its oil was used for wounds of the head. Jaundice was treated with botanical specimens that were yellow in colour. Lungwort with the suggestive shape of its leaves was used for respiratory conditions. Paracelsus was the doctrine's populariser. The arrival of the orchid had medical possibilities. Its appearance obviously suited it for treatment of conditions of the testicle.

In July 1736 a shabby foreigner who spoke no English arrived in London with a giant mission. Carl Linnaeus saw plants that had no like in his native Sweden. The variety of lilies included the eight-foot-high Lilium Superbum whose stems culminated in up to forty speckled orange flowers. The first tropical orchids brought from the Caribbean were in flower. Linnaeus was already author of *Systema Naturae* which proposed a new system for classification of plants. The taxonomy was based on the stamens and pistils in each specimen. The previous classificatory system used a variety of traits that ranged across shape, fruit, seed and habitat. Its advantage was that it posited a concept based on the species as a taxonomic unit. But it was inaccessible to any kind of layman. Linnaeus retained the unit of the species as his base but selected just one factor as the classificatory distinguisher. He named the stamens "husbands" and the pistils "wives". Under this scrutiny flowering plants fell into twenty-three classes and the natural world could be summarised in a few tables.

Linnaeus was a man possessed of an ambition without limit. "I brought the natural sciences to their highest peak," he announced, a declaration that had truth to it but no modesty. His meeting with Philip Miller at the Chelsea Physic Garden was turbulent and argumentative. Miller stormed out but tempers were soothed over glasses of wine that evening in a tavern. In Oxford Linnaeus was dismissed by a professor as "the man who has thrown all botany into confusion". The condescension of the connoisseurs of England was part-based on the fact that the Swede had seen seeds but few actual flowers. He rebutted his critics by identifying a flower he had never seen via its stamens and pistils. In Linnaeus' telling of the story his professorial host offered to split his salary with him that he might remain in Oxford and "under tears and kisses to live and die with him". Linnaeus left England in August, his bags packed with dried specimens, cuttings and seeds from America.

* * * *

The second leg of Andrea Wulf's tale is trade. Linnaeus had a preference for belittling his rivals by giving their names to plants of unpleasantness. A small and smelly little weed became Siegesbeckia in his system because a scientist called Johann Georg Siegesbeck had criticised his work in public. English good taste was also repulsed by the sexual metaphors used by the self-described "King of Botanists". "The bridal bed" and more earthy terms reduced botany to a carnival of reproduction. America by contrast, a place without access to catalogues of weight, welcomed the new system for its simplicity. John Bartram was a horticulturalist in Philadelphia who had a forty-year trading relationship in seeds with Peter Collinson, a London merchant whose family business had started in cloth.

Bartram built up a business that shipped seeds by the thousand to England. On the eastern side of the Atlantic it was financed by a subscription scheme priced at five guineas a box. Collinson was the vendor who stayed at home and sold "Bartram's boxes" of botanical wonders. Bartram was the adventurer wandering into unexplored territory in search of new plants. America's vastness was ripe for his plant-hunting travels. Collinson's clientele was a network of largely aristocratic buyers. Each year he would visit the Duke of Bedford's Woburn Abbey, the Earl of Jersey's Middelton Park in Oxfordshire and the Duke of Richmond's Goodwood

House in Sussex. His favourite was Thorndon in Essex, seat of the 8th Baron Petre. The Goodwood estate had been expanded from two hundred to eleven thousand acres and needed trees. Orders came for a hundred conifers at a time.

Collinson advised Bartram from a distance and the American set off to explore the Delaware river for the seeds, cones and acorns desired by his English collectors. Collinson sent him instructions and a compass for "exact observations of the course of thee river". Collinson regarded himself the social superior with a large knowledge of the colony he had never seen. His colleague would require a spare horse, baskets on both sides, linen, insect nets. "Be sure have some good covering of skins over the baskets, to keep out the rain" ran the somewhat condescending advice.

Collinson used his contacts to assist Bartram in his travels. Many of the wealthy land-owners of Virginia had visited Europe on the Grand Tour and letters of introduction facilitated Bartram on a fifteen-day journey, in unceasing rain, to Williamsburg. On an Appalachian trip Bartram covered eleven hundred miles. The two partners frequently bickered. Bartram complained that he had been sent a "rotten mouldy" hat. Collinson admitted "My Cap, it's true, had a small Hole or Two" but "instead of giving it away I wish thee had sent it Mee back again. It would have served Mee Two or Three Years to have worn in the Country in Rainy Weather."

The relationship across the distance of geography, education and background lasted until Collinson's death in 1768. It can be summed up in a single line that the connoisseur on the English side wrote: "I Long the arrival of the Ship with the Seeds."

* * * *

The third strand of Andrea Wulf's account, bound in with science and commerce, is exploration. When the *Endeavour* set sail under

Captain Cook its complement included the star pupil of Linnaeus. Daniel Solander had met the British botanist Joseph Banks in the reading room of the British Museum. Solander, the opposite of his master in being sociable and universally liked, had settled in London in 1763. The two, Banks and Solander, sailed the globe together. The mission was ostensibly to observe the transit of Venus but its real object was to investigate the new continent, Terra Australis Incognita. The voyage made Banks a celebrity and, with the aid of Solander, he became the centre of the botanical establishment of Britain.

Banks had an advantage of wealth from estates in Lincolnshire. But his quest for knowledge was limitless. He was led by the example of his mother. "I have from my childhood, in conformity with the precepts of a mother void of all imaginary fear," he said, "been in the constant habit of taking toads in my hand, and applying them to my nose and face as it may happen. My motive for doing this very frequently is to inculcate the opinion I have held, since I was told by my mother, that the toad is actually a harmless animal; and to whose manner of life man is certainly under some obligation as its food is chiefly those insects which devour his crops and annoy him in various ways."

His mother moved to Paradise Row in Chelsea and Banks spent hours in Miller's Physic Garden. At the age of twenty-three he became a Fellow of the Royal Society and was its President for forty-one years. When asked if he would undertake the Grand Tour of Europe, the norm for young men of means, he replied "Every blockhead does that. My Grand Tour shall be one around the world." He put £10,000 into the voyage of the *Endeavour*. When he came to board his luggage took days to load. Case upon case were loaded with paper, presses, pigments, lenses, razors, knives, preserving chemicals, wax, salt, nets, trawls, hooks, microscopes and telescopes, guns and a hundred books for reference.

After the voyage that took in Brazil, Tahiti and New Zealand as well as Australia, he advised the King, George III, on the Royal Botanic Gardens at Kew. Under his direction botanists were sent worldwide to collect plants. The presence of acacia and eucalyptus is due to Banks. Eighty species of plants carry his name. His home in Soho Square was converted into a natural history salon where two hundred guests might turn up for a working breakfast. Twenty thousand books were displayed in the panelled room at the back of his house. His personal collection was augmented with the offer from the executors for Linnaeus's son Carl to sell him the entire collection. A thousand guineas was the price for three thousand books, thousands of minerals, insects and shells, and nineteen thousand dried and mounted plants. He supported financially the first attempt to make a geological map of Britain. He became a Baronet, a Foreign Honorary Member of the American Academy of Arts and Sciences, served for forty-two years as a Trustee of the British Museum and was made a Knight of the Order of the Bath.

This elder, distinguished Banks can be seen in Cardiff in a painting by William Parry. In a triple portrait he is with Solander and Omai, a Tahitian who had travelled to Britain. A relative owned the Edwinsford estate in the Cothi valley through marriage and Banks spent three months there in the summer of 1767. On September 15th he undertook a five-day journey on horseback through Llanwrtyd Wells, Llandrindod Wells and Brecon.

* * * *

When the time comes for author-speaker and members of the Cardiganshire Horticultural Society and the Ceredigion Historic Gardens Trust to disperse, sunset on a June night is still an hour away. The time of cloud and lightning has passed. After the rich tale of voyage, science and commerce the landscape around Gogerddan is cast in a new light that is both literal and figurative.

It is a place of inconceivable complexity at the joint hands of its natural and human makers. On one side of the road the ranks of greenhouses are laid out. Further down the road the laboratories for plant research abut their barn and farm outbuildings.

The squally heat has passed and the late evening is placid enough that the rill of the River Clarach is audible. Behind them is the slope of Gogerddan wood with its wide species mix. True to the currents of the time the formal garden of Gogerddan was swept away in 1780. The Ordnance Survey of 1887 recorded the presence of eleven greenhouses. The parkland that is the view on this summer's evening is a work of culture and legacy of the brother gardeners.

Nature for these pioneers had the capacity to astound. The arrival of the Venus flytrap caused a sensation. It seemed to bridge the gap between fauna and flora. To retain a capability for wonder is a strand of that elusive quality of happiness. The professor of psychology in Chicago locates it in several aspects of gardening. There is no shortage of technology at play in the range and distribution of products. But there is no machine intermediary between the practitioner and the activity. Trowel and rake do not suffer function collapse or battery failure. There is no time-tabling or limitation on slots or availability. The garden is there, whenever. Most of all the gardener works in a context. The human hand is small while nature is large and not over-friendly to gardens. Gardeners experience directly the results of their efforts.

The measurement of happiness is now regular, a part of the research area of hedonics. The Germans have never scored particularly highly in happiness despite being a rich nation. Andrea Wulf came to Britain from Hamburg. The city-dwellers of Germany live in flats that were built as such. Their windows fit, they have pipes that do not burst in the winter and they come with a base-of-building lock-up storage area. But they do not come with a garden, although usually a green square is nearby. Gardens exist for the much lower proportion of owner-occupied houses. Wulf shows a picture as example. A few pansies occupy a near-empty bed. The hedges are shaved with the precision of a ruler.

From that cultural background her arrival in the London of the mid-1990s was a shock. Newsagents were piled with magazines on gardening. Gardening centres were situated on the fringe of every town and ran into the thousands. "I could not believe how obsessed the British were with their gardens," she says. There is even a condition known as plant bereavement. That is Europe versus Britain; so close, so different.

June 2016: Gogerddan

An Occasional Flash of Silliness

"Mistrust a man who never has an occasional flash of silliness". The words, unusual for a public monument, are carved in the stone of a public seat large enough for twelve people. The centre of the seat features a three-foot-high statue of an early-style diving suit. Winchester Cathedral also has a small statue of a man in a diving suit. That diver was a hero. Beginning in 1906 William Walker worked in total darkness under water beneath the cathedral for six hours a day. At depths of up to twenty feet he used his bare hands to feel his way through the cloudy, muddy water. It took him six years to excavate flooded trenches and fill them with bags of concrete. His work halted the subsidence of the building's walls. Walker died aged forty-nine in the great flu of 1918. This diver's outfit, carved in sandstone, was worn by Gerald Hugh Tyrwhitt-Wilson, 14th Baron Berners. He wore it to walk the town of Faringdon by daylight.

Faringdon is in a full flourish of Spring after successive waves of light rain and is the very picture of an older England. The Old Town Hall stands on its nine stone pillars from the seventeenth century. It has served at various times as court and prison, fire station and library. The pubs in the square are reliably called the Bell and the Old Crown. The Old Crown has a fine wooden gate and courtyard which was the place for billeting by Royalist cavalry in 1644. A Union Jack blows in the breeze on top of the stumpy tower of All Saints. The church has, a board proudly says, its mention in the Domesday Book. A signpost points out a footpath over the fields to the village of Thrupp. This is the Faringdon of the Vale of the White Horse rather than that of Devon. The buildings look as though they have been living with ivy and wallflower for centuries, which they probably have.

"What do people do in the Faringdon of today?" I wonder. "They sleep" a resident tells me. Once, she tells me, the town hosted twenty-two hostelries. The size of the cattle market was so great as to flood the whole of the town centre and beyond. The location was crucial. East-west it was Bath to London and the north-south axis is revealed in its name, Southampton Road. Now Swindon has the car plant and the business parks, Didcot has the power station and the fast train to Paddington, Oxford has the high-paying jobs. If people only come back to Faringdon to sleep it still has its beauty and its most famous resident, Lord Berners. A local organisation in his memory is called the Pink Pigeons Trust. Berners was not alone as a man of wealth in having birds dyed to a colour of his fancying. His fellow spirit, Henry Cyril Paget, 5th Marquess of Anglesey, had a similar inclination.

Eccentricity has a special claim in the culture. Edith Sitwell, herself an honorary member of the tribe, wrote a book on the subject in 1933 that went on to sell and sell. She took pride in it as a national trait: "Eccentricity exists particularly in the English because of that peculiar knowledge and infallibility that is the hallmark and the birthright of the British." It links to class and has a vein of superiority that runs through it. "Eccentricity is not, as dull people would have us believe, a form of madness. It is often a kind of innocent pride, and the man of genius and the aristocrat are frequently regarded as eccentrics because genius and aristocrat are entirely unafraid of and uninfluenced by the opinions and vagaries of the crowd." Lesser folk are treated with lesser kindness. A millionaire may be eccentric where a poor person is certifiable.

A privilege of wealth is the ability to buy isolation. The master of the moonwalk had many precursors in Britain. Charles Paget Wade bought Snowshill Manor in the Cotswolds in a wholly unmodernised condition with the house hidden behind nettles and giant thistles. He lived alone with just candles and oil lamps. The owner of two thousand costumes, he liked to dress up in them to the surprise of guests like John Betjeman and Virginia Woolf.

The aristocracy has always had a liking for animals, often preferring them to humans. The 8th Earl of Bridgewater had silver collars with the family crest made for his cats and dogs. His dining companions were his two favourite dogs, Bijoun and Biche. His footmen tied linen napkins around their necks and placed them in front of monogrammed plates. In Paris his coach would carry eight dogs. When nature called footmen would hold umbrellas over them as they discharged their natural functions in the Bois de Boulogne.

The 2nd Lord Rothschild also entertained dogs to dinner. He trained a team of zebras to pull his carriage and was to be seen riding a giant tortoise. The forward motion was achieved by a cabbage leaf on a piece of string being waved a few inches ahead of the tortoise's nose. He was also a formidable scientific collector, working up to fourteen hours a day. His team assembled a collection of two thousand stuffed animals, a greater number of birds, a thousand reptiles, three hundred thousand beetles and two and a quarter million insects. His name has been left on a type of giraffe, the *Giraffa camelopardalis rothschildi*. His carriage was certainly the only one to pass down Pall Mall and into Buckingham Palace to be pulled by zebras. Queen Alexandra was delighted.

Retainers were no disadvantage when it came to cultivating habits of particularity. Sir Tatton Sykes of Sledmere Hall left his home in layers of overcoats and trousers of different sizes. If he became overheated, he would discard layers until the eventual temperature was to his liking. The local arrangement was that every coat or pair of trousers returned to Sledmere Hall earned a meal and a shilling in payment. As for personal appearance, a Lord

Rokeby grew a beard so long it reached to his knees and a moustache so long he could sweep it back over his ears.

Idiosyncratic habits are not necessarily a diversion from accomplishment. A scion of a long aristocratic lineage had a large collection of Meccano – a universal metal building kit for children – and built a model of the Forth Rail Bridge. He enjoyed brick-laying and would add water to the finest of clarets. He worked in London his whole life but travelled just once on the underground. He liked the Vivien Leigh and Laurence Olivier film *The Hamilton Woman* so much he watched it over a hundred times. He had a collection of hundreds of butterflies who were chloroformed and pinned to a hard surface. He knew that cigars were bad for him so rationed himself to eight or nine a day. That is the giveaway that distinctive private habits, as in the case of Winston Spencer Churchill, need not preclude the highest public service.

In Faringdon, Lord Berners was an aesthete but also an accomplished composer, writer and artist. He had an aesthetic preference that a meal comprise food of similar colour. Stravinsky on a visit reported that a meal might consist of beet soup, lobster, strawberry and tomato. The birds on Berners' land would be changed not just to pink but to other shades to suit his mood. For composition and music-making he had a piano keyboard installed inside his Rolls Royce. Another account calls it a portable clavichord strapped beneath the seat.

Berners played on the borders of the acceptable. A large and unmistakably phallic folly was put up in the garden to celebrate his long-term lover. A visitor inscribed herself in the visitors' book as *Tempteuse de Serpents,* snake temptress. The Marchesa Luisa Casati was to be sighted with a living python neck-wrap and pageboys dipped in gold paint. Berners was a musician of gifts. Serge Diaghilev of the Ballets Russes stormed into the rooms of his collaborator shouting "*Je vous défends de faire de la peinture! Je vous le défends!*" "I forbid you to paint pictures! I forbid you!"

Berners had written the score for *The Triumph of Neptune* then given up music in favour of painting.

Berners' social life is a walk through the arts of his time – he died in 1950 aged sixty-six. He was acquainted with Max Beerbohm, Siegfried Sassoon, Lord Beaverbrook, Clive Bell, Evelyn Waugh, the Sitwells, H. G. Wells, Alice Astor, William Walton, Cecil Beaton, Gertrude Stein, Salvador Dali, George Balanchine, Frederick Ashton, Margot Fonteyn and Isaiah Berlin. It is more of a surprise since his family was upper-class, English, practically-minded, sporty and frosty. "Clever people" in his family were objects for suspicion. He himself said: "I have never made a point of explaining to myself why I like certain things. You must remember that I am a Victorian and good Victorians never analysed their motives."

As for the diving suit and helmet now immortalised in stone in Faringdon it had a role in the short history of surrealism in Britain. Berners wore it for a walk around the town in a wager with Salvador Dali. On a spring day in 1936, Dali had visited a diving shop in the south east of England and asked to be fitted for a deep-sea diving suit. When the salesman enquired how deep he intended to venture, the Spaniard replied that his dive was to be into the depths of the human subconscious.

At the International Surrealist Exhibition held that year at the New Burlington Galleries in London Dali had worn the suit. It became apparent that he was suffocating after a bout of arm-waving which was at first taken to be part of the show. He grappled to loosen the rivets that held the sphere tight. He was saved from public death either by Berners or the surrealist Edward James with the help of a billiard cue. Other versions of the tale say more dully that his life was saved by a plain workman with a spanner.

Back at the public seat in Faringdon, Berners may have been subject to his occasional flashes of silliness but it is hard not to warm to a man who wrote a verse called "Auto-epitaph".

"Here lies Lord Berners
   One of the learners
   His great love of learning
   May earn him a burning
   But praise to the Lord
   He seldom was bored"

June 2016: Faringdon

The Map-makers

Maps are made for purposes and each map has its own intention. The maps that accompanied January's conference on the Anthropocene were intended to show the deep workings of time. The government of the German Democratic Republic made maps which falsified the borders of neighbouring countries. Their purpose was to delude and confuse would-be escapees. Soldier-scholar Jonathon Riley spoke at Cardiff's National Museum at the time of the centenary of the battle for Mametz Wood. He brought with him close-up campaign illustrations of the terrain. Both sets of maps required the professional eye to read their significance. The eye of the geomorphologist becomes that of an innocent layman when it turns to the map that is filled with meaning for the soldier. The same becomes the case in reverse.

The great nodes of communication that link the digital highway, the server farms, have a habit of disappearing from digital maps. There is a tradition to this. In 1927 Prime Minister Stanley Baldwin decreed: "No work of defence shall appear on any map on sale to the general public." During the Cold War five thousand "key points" of Britain vanished from maps. The places included mines, quarries and mills. Hughenden Manor is also a place of maps that were hidden. Like the code-breakers of Bletchley Park it was home to activities in the Second World War that were kept secret for long afterwards.

The location of Hughenden Manor is a lush green valley with High Wycombe, a warren of roundabouts, a few minutes' distance away. Cranes from the town's building sites are visible between the trees. The Manor itself is high on one side of the valley with a wide view from its garden terrace. The church, much lower, is older and made of the flint and stone of the Chilterns. It is a morning for a practice ringing of its bells and they peal for an hour. The whole scene is classic National Trust territory and there is a deep aspect of satisfaction in it.

The Manor is larger, more solid and squarer by a degree greater than the word suggests. The interior is also unexpected. The larger rooms of ground and upper floors have been refurbished as pure Victoriana in detail, decoration and smell. A small stair to the side of the entry area drops to an under-floor which has a different story to tell. Hughenden Manor played a key role in the Second World War. It was a place for the making of maps.

The maps of wartime came in every form and size. The aircrew who flew on bombing raids carried maps made of mulberry tissue. If their aircraft were downed and they were mobile they had maps for escape. The maps showed in fine detail the border between Germany and Switzerland and the best route for crossing. Other maps cover areas that can be large or small. The Czechoslovak Ministry of Information published as a poster the map that the Gestapo made of the village of Lidice. Its full extent was just a mile. The massacre and destruction of the village was prepared in fine detail. That was a map for the execution of atrocity. In contrast a map from the wars in the Balkans was one of salvation. Two map-makers in Sarajevo, Suada Kapic and Miran Norderland, made a survival map. Their city was ringed by Serb tanks, artillery and rocket-launchers. Their map for the inhabitants showed the tunnels, the special corridors for protection from sniper fire, the parks that had been converted into vegetable gardens.

The map is not the territory. Mike Parker in his book *The Wild Rover* described drawing a five-mile circle around his house. It looked too great a challenge to explore. He closed the circle to a radius of three miles. It was utterly disorientating, comprising valleys, farms and woods he knew nothing about. The world's bigness starts a few feet from a front door and is outside any map. The world is not its map.

Captain Winrich Behr in the middle of the Battle for Stalingrad was flown to headquarters, the Wolfsschanze. He described to the leadership, from his first-hand knowledge, the situation that faced the Sixth Army on the ground. Hitler turned back to the great map in the bunker that was dotted with little flags that showed positions from months before. Where the flags represented troops by the thousand, the reality was that there were divisions with just a few hundred men surviving. Hitler reprised his message of a brilliant counter-stroke. Behr knew that it was over. "I saw then that he had lost touch with reality. He lived in a fantasy world of maps and flags. It was the end of all my illusions about Hitler. I was convinced that we would now lose the war." The map is not the territory.

Maps are politics. The nature of the projection can shrink or magnify the significance of territories. Alaska is one-fifth the size of Brazil and assumes dimensions that are similar. Greenland can be shown to be much the same size as Africa. In *Officer and Laughing Girl* Vermeer painted a map on the wall in an exact reproduction. Its title was *The New and Accurate Topography of All Holland and West Friesland* and it was printed by Willem Blaeu as a piece of commissioned propaganda to celebrate the war of the Dutch for independence. The map contains three dozen ships as markers of the power of the Dutch East India Company.

Michael Herr opens his book of reportage on Vietnam, *Despatches*, stretched out on a bed in Saigon. He gazes at an ancient map on the wall, buckled in the heat, that has been made in Paris. It shows a Vietnam that no longer exists. The country is divided into its old territories of Tonkin, Annam and Cochin China. Not a single public map of today in Ecuador shows the same borders as maps in its neighbour Colombia. The Institute for Peace and Economics has its own map of the world. It uses twenty-three different measures of instability to construct a Global Peace Index.

All fiction can be reduced to seven plots. One archetype is the quest and the map is a crucial part. The journeys of Jim Hawkins and Long John Silver, Indiana Jones, Robert Langston and Bilbo Baggins are fuelled by maps. Maps are the centre of the plot of *The English Patient*. Geoffrey Clifton pretends that his plane has been a wedding present. It is revealed to be a government plane and its mission is aerial photography of North Africa. Cinema's most famous map is a dynamic narrative that lasts fifty seconds. *Casablanca* opens with the route of escape, the sea journey from Marseilles to Oran and overland to Fez and Casablanca. The map is double-exposed over footage of real refugees on foot, bicycle and horse-drawn cart.

The twentieth century was the highpoint for the printed map. The new virtual maps are stripped of rich detail and selective in their features. The Ordnance Survey showed prehistoric mounds, weirs, disused railways. The layering of time on a topography was represented over centuries. In a digital version the town of Tewkesbury in Gloucestershire has lost its great Romanesque abbey but gained a Golf and Country Club.

The digital map was born at midnight on January 5th 1980. Coordinated Universal Time was determined from an average of more than two hundred atomic clocks across the world. Geopolitical stationing was a child of the military. The Cold War required a technology to intercept incoming Soviet ballistic missiles and to direct missiles of attack to their targets. The USA Department of Defence oversees the system and the monitoring stations that ensure the satellites work belong to the National Security Agency.

This new era of map-reading is of fascination to psychology. The navigation skill of the Polynesians of the Pacific is known to be remarkable. GPS presupposes the user as the centre of the map and the data is reduced to one fixed point in relation to another. But the Polynesians combined a density of perceptual information with a grasp of the relational movement between two fixed points and a third moving one, the parallax view. Science knows that the hippocampus is the brain region that is specialised to navigate the spatial environment. Map-reading, drawing on orientation and navigational skills, can cause the hippocampus to grow in the formation of more neural pathways. Researchers at University College London found that grey matter in the brains of taxi drivers grows and adapts as they store ever more detailed mental maps of the city. MRI scans reveal taxi drivers to have larger hippocampi than other people.

McGill University in Canada conducted three studies on the effects of using GPS devices on the brain. They found that excessive reliance on technology may lead to atrophy in the hippocampus with age. The risk of cognitive disease may rise. Alzheimer's disease affects the hippocampus first before any other part of the brain. The University of Tokyo asked three groups of people to find their way through an urban environment on foot with different aids. Their study found that the group with the GPS walked more slowly, made more stops, walked farther, made more errors and took longer to reach their destination. When asked to draw a map their knowledge of the terrain, topography, and the routes they had taken was poor. The size of the device screen excludes a representation where location and destination both feature.

The destination of the map-makers of Hughenden was Germany and their purpose was destruction. The cellar floor of the Manor comprises a series of bare-brick rooms which document the wartime activity. The working conditions were characteristic in their Spartan rigour. The upper rooms contained table after table with a standard angle-poise light. The floors were without carpets and heating came from a fireplace. The fingers that held their pencils were often chilly. A recreated room with a bare bunk has information that gives the context of wartime deprivation. In the Great War food was so precious that throwing rice at weddings was prohibited. It was made unlawful to feed pigeons and stray dogs. Even in peacetime conditions were hard. In the winter of 1927 coal was tightly rationed and most people were cold all the time. The rooms contain newspapers casually displayed. It is history as experienced in its first unfurling. The front page of the *Daily Herald* reads "Axis Is in Full Retreat" and below "Rommel's Deputy Killed: Other Generals Taken."

Another newspaper was made in Hughenden. Britain's shortage of cartographers for war was acute. Artists, graphic designers, architects and cartoonists were assembled. A house newspaper was published with the cartoonists lending their talents. Eventually the shortage of paper in the wartime economy terminated the newspaper. The processes of map-making for use in the air were elaborate. Painting was done by hand on transparent foil. The foils were transferred to thin photo-sensitive plates. Chemical treatments were applied before they were placed in the lithographic printing press. Different machines printed different colours. The machines themselves had been requisitioned from across Britain. Secrecy was inbuilt. Sealed packages were collected from the Manor to be taken to Bomber Command.

The map-making at Hughenden came into public light as late as 2005. As at Bletchley Park the Official Secrets Act had a potency that lasted for decades. The visitors today are few in number and inclined to talk. A volunteer steward recounts the history of his own family. His father never spoke of the war but had been pressed for his memories from North Africa and Italy after its invasion. The episode with a Polish Division at Monte Cassino had been written down and sent tentatively to the Imperial War Museum. The Museum replied that it was part of the war of which they had had no prior material. That father lived to tell his tale. Another visitor tells of his father who had been in London's East End in the time of 1930s Depression. He had seen promise in work in the rubber plantations of Malaya. That hope of self-betterment led to captivity and death in the making of the Burma Railway.

A short film has recorded the voices of the veterans of Hughenden in their old age. The bombing of Germany in the later part of the war was relentless. Every mission had its origin in the sealed packages with the contents that were made in these rooms. Some voices of the participants have been caught for posterity. Leonard Chance: "We tried to minimise the indiscriminate bombing." Kathlyn Hudson: "I used to put my hands together to pray. Please, God, don't let this kill any children." The speaker who made the maps that guided the bombers pauses and adds: "Of course He didn't listen."

June 2016: Hughenden, Buckinghamshire

A Citizen's Guide to
the European Union

The referendum is eight days away and unsurprisingly the Hong Kong Theatre at the London School of Economics' Clement Building is packed. An expert is to hand. Chris Bickerton is author of *The European Union: A Citizen's Guide*. It is a book small enough in size to be droppable in a pocket, but big in substance. From the podium he acknowledges the help and domestic support in its making. He was confident that the referendum would be called for September and its move to a midsummer date has meant a compressed time scale. The shrinking of the timescale by three months is serious for any author. For an academic, with the particular rhythm of the profession's year, it is especially so.

Bickerton is a reminder as to why we have universities. His is a cool, succinct, probing intelligence, far remote from the last months of public hyperbole, selectiveness and side-taking. The European Union he presents is a hazy mirage. Viewed more closely in the company of this authoritative voice, it does not get any clearer. But it is an improvement on the clamour of the campaigns. He explains the reason. The Stayers were warned by focus groups not to make mention of the Union itself. The Union is a vote-loser, which explains its utter absence over the months past.

Bickerton's perspective is precisely the reverse of those who claim loss of sovereignty. The Commission itself, through the lens of the political scientist, has been leaching power for a long period. "The Commission is weak because it does not have the powers of implementation and ratification," he states. Those who trumpet a super-state, trampling on national democratic freedoms, exaggerate its power and authority. They ignore the small size of the EU administration and the central role played by national governments. Authority rests in the European Council and every participant is there by dint of a process conducted by a national state.

Bickerton has small truck for the misty myth of a continent merging its many nationalities. The Easyjet model of an Italian pilot employed by a Greek entrepreneur taking the English to their French retreats does not extend far. The overwhelming bulk of Europeans live as, and where, their parents did. "We live in national societies," he says, "the intermingling is very shallow."

His lecture and his book have a purpose. "My goal has always been to describe the European Union as it is and not as we may wish it to be." The Union is a way of life and those with memories of the time before are few. But it does not excite. Its spokespeople are dull and its buildings all look the same. Its structure is unknown to all except its workers. "We think of it with a sense of unhappy fatalism," he says. It is a genuine puzzle as to why it has achieved such a distance from popular sentiment. It is in part aesthetic. We like a politics that has a dash to it, with a dose of excitement and visual stimulus. What we get are identikit men going in and out of meetings. Its behaviour is not how Britain likes its politics. The verbal fisticuffs are eased away or conducted privately.

In June 2014 one Chancellor and three Prime Ministers climbed into a small rowing boat on a Swedish lake. In a revealing simile the Briton declares his life jacket to be unnecessary as he can swim "like a Labrador". The Union offers little to look at, so a boat outing gets amplified. The Labour party has hardly featured on television. The cream of old Britain has led; the voices are those of Eton, Balliol and Sandhurst. Bickerton too is located in an old Britain as a Fellow of Queens' College, Cambridge is bound to be.

But he does detail and numbers, areas where television is unhappy. The Commission's headcount is a little below twenty-five thousand. The USA has a population around a third less than that of the EU; its Department of Commerce alone employs forty-four thousand. But the Union is its own enemy in structuring complexity. It is a rare voter next week who could even guess at what distinguishes the European Council from the Council of Ministers. The author in his book puts in a friendly "Still Reading? Good" and he is on to Ecofin, Agrifish, Coreper, parts I and II. He describes exactly the working methods of the Antici diplomats. Bickerton is a rebuttal to those who insist the cybersphere will reveal everything. The Cambridge scholar tells it plainly in a crisp book where the Internet does not.

Institutions have their origins and Bickerton goes back to Monnet, Schuman and Delors. Chunks of recent European experience are unknown to us. In 1996 rates of interest in Bulgaria exceeded three hundred percent. In 2013 Slovenia's three main banks, all state-owned, collapsed. Some figures are straightforward. Labour mobility, Europeans at work in a state that is not their own, stands at three percent. Ninety-seven percent of the total working population lives at home. But history is also complicated. Economic integration is variable and Europe is compared with CARICOM, SACU, CACM and EACM, not to mention the bilateral agreements with Andorra, San Marino and Turkey.

Bickerton touches deftly on the cultures that make the coalition of Europe. For the Mediterranean nations Brussels has a double identity. Firstly, it is rejection of rule by soldiers. Within living memory Spain, Greece and Portugal have all been dictatorships. More importantly, the EU is government of order and even-handedness. The Mediterranean wants government on the principles of Max Weber. "Spain is the problem, Europe the solution", said Ortega de Gasset on his country's accession in 1986.

De Gasset is his country's greatest philosopher. Europe is a philosophical furnace in a way that the USA is not. When Germany speaks of the EU, it is the voice of Hegel. The Commission is pure

Descartes. Bickerton homes in on a debate between two living thinkers, Jürgen Habermas and Wolfgang Streeck. The maintenance of Europe's high standard of living and the extensive regime of social rights require, in the Habermas view, a supranational state. For Streeck: "Europe is more heterogeneous and more divided than ever. Differences between national societies are acute." Habermas versus Streeck is a rerunning of Fichte versus Herder.

Culture precedes politics. A six-minute walk away from this hall is Lincoln's Inn Fields and the former home on its north side of Sir John Soane. The house is also home to Hogarth's *Election* series of paintings. It is politics as raucous, noisesome, public and vital. Art does not teach but it makes the metaphors that we follow. France does Liberty storming the barricades and Britain does Hogarth.

That meeting of the four premiers in the rowing boat on the Swedish lake was a tussle as to who would be next President of the Commission, a power in fact lost to the European Parliament. Had more noise emanated from the edifice of the EU there might have been less protest from Britain. The fact of a portable Parliament was not compromise; it was asinine. Bickerton cites the German sociologist Claus Offe who identifies the core dilemma, greater powers versus public resistance. "Europe is 'entrapped'" he says, "unable to move forward, it cannot move backwards either."

Bickerton the political scientist ends with a sober diagnosis of the times. In Britain allegiance to party by class has evaporated. To try to beat UKIP on nostalgia is not enough. "Political competition is increasingly structured around twin poles of populism and technocracy," says the political scientist. Books, and universities, are there to make us see the world more truly. The vote on June 23rd is a choice between the status quo and the new, the dimensions of which are entirely unknown. Book and lecture have a rattling sense of certainty, even as far as casting a doubt that perhaps the status quo might not deserve the shattering.

But Bickerton leaves one question hanging. Decisions on health and education, foreign alliances and military campaigns are not in the domain of the Commission. In its absence, he asks, who will its excoriators find instead to blame?

June 2016: London

They Are Obsessed by Fear

My first job was in the telecommunications industry. The duties were various. At ten in the morning the canteen manager would call for all hands to make two hundred pieces of toast for the staff. I went on the next year to the head office of the Bell Telephone Company in Pennsylvania. I was of interest as the only twenty-one-year-old, the only foreigner, and the only white staff member. The permanent canteen employees were of the kindest nature imaginable. The duties for a busboy were not demanding. The diners left behind a myriad of newspapers. My five weeks coincided with the inexorable last weeks, then days, of the Watergate saga that had been rumbling for two years. The copies of *The Philadelphia Enquirer* which I had to clear away made riveting reading day on day.

I went on to work in logistics, the automotive industry and civic emergency planning. In the first I delivered the Christmas post competently and at the second counted piles of engine components on a Sunday in a car factory. In Berlin the City Senate maintained warehouses of food, the precise quantity kept secret, lest Russia should repeat the blockade of 1948. The boxes of canned goods were piled high to the ceiling. A day spent in their shifting was grimy and arduous. The time came eventually, when work was to be no longer a short term means to fund the next youth hostel, Interrail or Greyhound ticket. It had to be the real thing.

When I arrived at Britain's tenth largest company it had a computer. The installation occupied much of its own chamber and could be visited for special reasons. It had double doors and a specialist filtration system against the danger of dust. The company's total processing capability was less than that of a smartphone. The organisation's information ran on paper flows. But typed words had a cost, so there was a strong management bias in favour of resolution by personal encounter and telephone. The division in which I worked had only a dozen products but each came in four forms and fifteen different sizes. One of the documents I had to refer to regularly was the great file of transfer prices. The company's microbiologists and biochemists were in Surrey, the manufacturers were in Singapore and the Sussex Coast, the marketers were in London and the users, the customers of my section, across Arabia. Even to a trainee's eye, quite where the company yielded its profit was anyone's guess.

Taxation is a mix of allure, complexity and bewilderment over its detail. But it has a paradox at its heart. The world has two hundred tax jurisdictions that are state-based. States have a commonality of language at their core, although not always. They are geographically contiguous, although not always. Kaliningrad, for instance, is separated from Russia.

But economic activity, at least some of it and always growing, is not bothered with language unity, kin or border. The division of work by specialisation, its allocation to those best able to undertake it, is remarkable. Bertolt Brecht sang in its favour when he ended *The Caucasian Chalk Circle* and his setting was a communist collective. The results have been a boon for consumers but a headache for tax-collectors. Among individual payers of tax themselves the only binding conviction is that others are not paying enough, but that they themselves are doing their share. The top one percent of Income Tax payers in Britain accounts for twenty-seven percent of the total. Income Tax in its totality barely exceeds the total for value-added tax. In fact, the shift in the relative balance from indirect to direct taxation has been going on for decades.

In this zone of contention Gabriel Zucman is an economist and does the real numbers. He is a visitor from the University of California, Berkeley, and the subject of his talk at the Hong Kong Theatre in the London School of Economics is *The Hidden Wealth of Nations*. It is the same as the title of his book of 2015 from Chicago's University Press. Zucman has researched numbers that are big and global. World assets nudge around a hundred trillion dollars. About eight percent of assets is held offshore, much quite legitimately. The tax loss is one hundred and ninety billion dollars. There are many offshore havens but Zucman points to the three that dominate. They are Switzerland, the Virgin Islands and Luxembourg.

My neighbours in the lecture hall are two young summer school students from Beijing. "We are interested in this," says the one next to me. She does look very young. I am too polite to mention recent news. The release of the Panama Papers, with their mass of shell company details, has not been flattering to the rulers of China.

Gabriel Zucman is a scholar, which means rigour in the presentation of data. The evidence is not infallible, he says, but nonetheless he and the academics who have preceded him have their models. He has a slide that shows a selection of nations and the proportion of their financial assets that is held overseas. Russia comes in at number one with a remarkable fifty percent. These are large numbers, world output being in the region of eight hundred trillion dollars – that is an eight followed by twelve zeros. This money is not bad by definition. Zucman makes the basic distinction between private capital and that held by corporate treasuries. The titans of tech are now always the first to be cited. Google's entirely open and legitimate cash balance is given as an example.

There are concerted movements by governments underway to resolve the disjunction between sovereign jurisdictions and international economic organisation. The acronyms of the USA's

FATCA and BEPS are explained. Bank records are shareable across borders. Technology now has the capability for a global asset registry akin to national land registries. The Common Reporting Standard involves over one hundred countries but that still leaves a lot out.

Zucman adds a note from history. 1791 was the date of the first land registry. The country was France at a time when land essentially was wealth. As for privacy concerns Zucman looks to Norway. The wealth tax records are in the public domain and not in an archive but online. Type in a name and the record is there.

He is careful in his geographical distinction. Wealth management is a speciality of Singapore and Luxembourg. The Caymans are a centre for shadow banking and treasury management for US corporations. Ten percent of American equities is owned offshore. The anomaly in the aggregated balance sheets of all the nations is considerable. Assets and liabilities should be equal and are not; the imbalance, the preponderance of liabilities over assets, represents the wealth that is hidden. But he reports a promising trend. As a percentage year on year the disparity is dropping.

Zucman looks too to history for the foundations of the treatment of taxation across borders. In 1920 the League of Nations asked four economists to draw up principles where borders were involved. The system of transfer pricing, which provided my lists of working figures a half-century on, was based on a simple notion. The price was set at the level as if it were from another supplier. It worked fine for a staple, says Zucman, such as coffee. As a base principle it is lost when faced with intellectual property where there are no reference prices. The issue when the League of Nations addressed it was a small proportion of economic activity. Now thirty-five percent of US corporate income is abroad. A multilateral system is lacking in place of bilateral agreements that run into the thousands. As recently as

1980 General Electric had $4.8bn revenue outside the USA and now it is $65bn. Its tax department employs nine hundred.

Zucman's audience is predominately young. A much older member has come prepared for his question in the post-lecture session. He has quotations from the *New Internationalist* and the *New Statesman*. Bank accounts, he declares in manifesto more than question, are not the full story, not by any means. Two billion people work in the informal or shadow or grey economy. The man on the floor says that experts have calculated it should add a tenth to the domestic product of Britain. A paper by Friedrich Schneider on the Eurozone has put the grey sector at four percent. Eighty-four percent of transactions worldwide are in cash. According to the official tally Uber drivers in the capital of Europe, Brussels, are averaging twenty-eight Euros a day.

Taxation has its commentators in droves. The rates system goes back to the Poor Law Act of 1572. Property is easy to tax because it sits there. It is a system out of kilter with the retail rush from bricks to clicks. The British Retail Consortium has floated an idea that tax be based on energy consumption, so that online retailers pay the social costs of their fleets of vans and couriers. The most common plea is for simplicity over complexity of staggering dimensions. Distortion is built in to the fact of different treatment of a pound sterling depending on context. GDP is the product of capital and labour and both sources of income should be taxed in the same way. Business taxes on profits, which are an accounting convention, should be replaced by tax of cash outflows which are not and are, like PAYE, chargeable at source.

These writers too have evidence to hand that productivity and real wages for employees correlate to lower tax rates on profits. Companies are substantial legal entities but the value of their output is geographically evanescent. For decades the biggest building on the Pontarddulais Road into Swansea was a heaving snack food factory. It went in 2005, to be integrated into another sizeable factory in England. Its products are munched across Britain in the hundreds of millions. But its large physical installation has the lightest of corporate footprints on the actual soil of Britain. In 2009 all the intellectual property and "business functions and risk" went a-travelling and found a new home in Bern.

Writing on taxation is rarely neutral of politics. Zucman aspires to be the objective calculator of hidden wealth. His best counterpart in journalism is Nicholas Shaxson, whose press reports are substantially gathered together in his book *Treasure Islands*. The formation of subsidiaries was started in the 1920s by oil companies active in Persia. When Enron collapsed it had eight hundred and eighty-one offshore subsidiaries. Every one was incorporated in the remnants of the British Empire.

Shaxson explores the history of quite how the offshore phenomenon came about. It is not pure flight capital and kleptocracy. It had a kind of logic in its beginnings. The League of Nations treaty of 1928 was sincere in intention. It sought genuinely to mediate between the obligations to host countries, where an asset was performing an economic activity, and the owner countries. As the British dominions broke free, offshore seemed a sensible solution for territories too small for independent viability. At the end of 1959 the likes of Anguilla and Grand Turk held deposits of a couple of hundred million pounds. As a percentage of Britain's GDP, the role was miniscule. The Vietnam war played a part as government bonds skewed the US bond market. Thus the Eurobond emerged and the arrival on the financial scene of the Dutch Antillean islands.

Shaxson is a visitor to the territories that are British but totally non-British. The closest are the Channel Islands. An insider who went public said that in a single quarter in 2009 the City of London received net financing of three hundred and thirty-two billion dollars from these tiny sources. Jersey's history is summarised in an article from the *Wall Street Journal*. The insider from the 1990s says that rates of tax ceased to apply. The wealthy, who sought residence, would send in lawyers to negotiate a flat sum for payment. An economy has gone from boat-building and cod-fishing to global finance player but is presided over "mostly by small-business owners and farmers. By and large they are totally out of their depth." Being British reassures. A former Senator in the islands says: "There is a kind of tatty credibility that clings to the public administration here, which comes from operating under the skirts of the establishment in London."

Good journalism has an eye for sharp detail. Intra-company pricing between subsidiaries is embedded in treaty and convention. It includes the litre of apple juice that costs two thousand dollars and the ballpoint pen that comes in at eight and a half thousand dollars. The stashing away of assets transcends ideologies. Shaxson cites estimates from South Korea that the Dear Leader to the North has around four billion stashed in Europe. He usefully tracks the distinction between domicile and resident back to the Empire. It was then a sensible way to treat an administrator who might spend decades in India. In 2006 *The Sunday Times* reported that fifty-four billionaires lived in Britain. Two-thirds of the combined tax they paid came from just one man, James Dyson.

Shaxson remembers the banks in their golden days. Royal Bank of Scotland gave a gold card and ten thousand pounds of unsecured credit to a Monty Slater in Manchester. Little Monty was a shih-tzu dog. As for the companies, Nevada, according to Shaxson, does not share tax or incorporation information with the Federal authorities. The state does not require a company to report where it conducts its business. The Caymans' company law is modelled on English law dating from 1862, but with some changes. Directors' names, even a company charter, are not required. The Accounting Standards Board sounds akin to the

Law Society or the General Medical Council. Not so: it is a private company with a registration in Delaware. A Caribbean building is home to twelve thousand companies but is a minnow. "An office at 1209 North Orange Street, Wilmington", writes Shaxson, "houses the grand total of two hundred and seventeen thousand companies".

The rules of taxation can be mad. Non-residential property in New York is depreciable over thirty-nine years. The rental income and the capital value can soar but the buildings, under the rules, make losses for ever. As for technology, Zucman says it is not ever going to catch the tubes of toothpaste that pass over borders impregnated with diamonds. As for these women and men at the top, they are as human as any in their strange homes. The Knightsbridge block that overlooks Hyde Park with its £136m Ukrainian-owned penthouse is plain chilly to an average eye. I have had just one glimpse into their psychology. In a sleek office next to Albany in Piccadilly I once spent an intriguing hour with an advisor to a clan whose assets were in the $7bn-$8bn range. "You have to understand," he said, "they are obsessed, by fear, fear of losing it."

June 2016: London

Among the Demonstrators

"Him? Oh, he's Satan!" This feels to be a first. It is certainly not usual to hear a wife referring to her husband in demonic terms. But relations between the two of them seem warm and she does not appear to be a Satanist herself. It is irony. This has been a day when smart people have gathered in common purpose. She is smart in appearance too in the way of Americans of wealth. She is cool and elegantly casual in summer-colour clothing. She is a tech player. There are only two cities in Europe, she says, where the serious tech guys gather. As her husband is with a hedge fund Berlin is a low-ranker for him. Only in London do money and software combine to suit both halves of a power couple. As for the devilish qualities of her husband, that has been her answer to the question from strangers: "What do you do?"

Our setting is a table above the Thames just down-river from Parliament. The normal rules of social propriety entail that strangers keep a small distance between themselves. But some events melt the norms of social convention. It happens when a heavy snowfall disrupts normal movement. It used to happen when Britain had strikes and was without power. It takes an exceptional event to create a sense of solidarity. So it has been today. Thirty thousand people have walked down Whitehall and thronged Parliament Square.

The group around this table is taking its tea after the hours in the sun. It has been a very British occasion. The weather has been warm, the faces of the police benign in expression. The police have their stresses but they know that the gathering of Hampstead's best is the least cause for alarm. It is a demonstration so those familiars, the Socialist Workers Party, have been out. True to tradition they are small in number but large in denunciation. The issue is Europe but also in keeping with tradition they have small interest in the specific issue. "Tories out! Tories out!" is the cry, but as their numbers hardly make double figures they are not making much impact. To be for the Union anyhow is to support the status quo. The occasion is curiously conservative. Speaker after speaker has pointed a finger rightward. The platform is set against Westminster Abbey, so the rightward finger is geographical not political. The object is Parliament. "We" thunder the voices, "are a parliamentary democracy!" The cheers are loud and repeated. It is a good day for Parliament, even if on a Saturday its inhabitants are elsewhere.

* * * *

Publishing is well-tuned to react with speed to events. It is only eight days since that Friday morning when a pivot of history swivelled. The first clump of books is half-written already. Later the big books of the history of 2016 will appear. It will not be easy to chart the line of how events unfurled. It has been a season of din. It has certainly been testament to a vibrant civic culture, the noise, turbulence and participation worthy of the time when Hogarth painted his views of the political process.

Whether anyone emerged better enlightened about the workings of the Union is doubtful. The first polls are out suggesting that not a mind was shifted since it all kicked off in the winter. The actual deeds of the Commission tend to be specific in intent and dull in nature. There is more spark in the revelation that a Leave leader's favourite character in fiction is Tyrion Lannister. "It's a stitch-up. It's the biggest stitch-up since the Bayeux tapestry", runs a piece of press copy intended to amuse more than enlighten.

The week since has had an air of the fictional Don Fabrizio Salina observing Garibaldi's unification of Italy. "Everything must change in order it may remain the same." The Common Agricultural Policy has been cause for bile for as long as anyone can remember. Within days *The Times* has a letter from the NFU President. Nothing, but nothing, must be permitted to change. *The Telegraph*'s star politician-writer wrote on June 26th: "There will still be intense and intensifying European cooperation and partnership in a huge number of fields: the arts, the sciences, the universities, and on improving the environment. EU citizens living in this country will have their rights fully protected, and the same goes for British citizens living in the EU. British people will still be able to go and work in the EU; to live; to travel; to study; to buy homes and to settle down. As the German equivalent of the CBI – the BDI – has very sensibly reminded us, there will continue to be free trade, and access to the single market." So free movement remains, not what the nay-sayers were led to believe.

Daniel Hannan in a television interview is of the view that freedom of movement is neither here nor there. Evan Davies, his interviewer, is left incredulous. "We've just been through three months of agony over immigration", he is gasping in sheer disbelief, "and the public has been led to believe that what they have just voted for is an end to immigration." Now a vote for change appears to be a vote for no change. On June 27th Richard Wyn Jones wrote his article *Why did Wales shoot itself in the foot in this referendum?*, one of the most read and shared of the last week. The coalition of the shires of old England with Margate, Spalding and Torfaen is surely not one that can hold.

* * * *

The historians of the future will have no shortage of voices from which to choose. There is a paradox to living in mass society. We live in groups of two to three hundred within states that comprise millions. Ann McElvoy first broached the subject in the *Evening Standard* in June. She was at a social gathering of Remainers. Not only did the group not know a single Out-er but she says they had a pride in it. The London commentators have been swift this week to visit the foreign lands that are their own country. Within a few days, the BBC's *Panorama* has been in Tipton and Nechells. The weekend's *Financial Times* and Bagehot of *The Economist* are both in Derby. A first camera was in Worcester. The interview ran:

"What do you think will change?"

"Everything."

"Like what?"

"Wages will go up."

Wages will not go up. In fact, in an import economy with its currency fifteen percent down prices will go up. Expectations are too high. Peter Hennessy is a voice of weight and used words of weight for a radio programme. "Thursday 23rd June 2016, European referendum day, scored a line across the page of British history. The incision was swift, the cut deep. The greatest adjustment in our lifetime, a caesura in our national history and our place in the world, a guillotine moment." The revelation to this long-term observer has been of "fissures in our society deeper and more jagged than I had fathomed."

So many discordant voices. So much reduction to a Manichean contest between good and ill. "A bonfire of red tape!" It sounds good but the detail means beef dosed with growth-enhancing hormones and chicken bleached with chlorine. The true restraints on economic liberty are home-grown in the form of planning restriction, miserable training and education expectations. "We beat the Germans in '45 and we've done it again," says the taxi driver in Lincoln, sniffing an air of metro-appeasement about his passenger in the back seat. "It's all our money!" is the response in the assisted areas on being pointed to the slew of projects carrying the blue Union symbol with its circle of stars. EU money comes with less political patronage than that from London, say the insiders, and with fewer strings attached.

Britain holds 24th position in the Union nations for number of doctors per head of population. Maybe we are younger and healthier. One in ten doctors is European-born, say the liberals. An MP addresses a public meeting in Peterborough and asks what the audience would be prepared to put at risk in order to leave. "Everything!" is the bellowed reply. Economics has been trounced by culture and culture goes deep. "The English are not intellectual," wrote George Orwell. "They have a horror of abstract thought, they feel no need for any philosophy or systematic 'worldview.'"

The seam that sniffs at big ideas in favour of pragmatism saw off republicanism, fascism and communism. It seems fanciful that memory of dictatorship, the reign of Cromwell, strikes so deep. But the Church of England is slack in theology. Edmund Burke liked his Britons' aversion to "pure reason", "abstract" principles. Pragmatism likes to cock a snook at authority. Orwell wrote of the songs of the First World War: "The only enemy they ever named was the sergeant-major."

In a recent book, *Democracy for Realists*, Christopher Achen and Larry Bartels recount how people in New Jersey were significantly less likely to vote to re-elect President Woodrow Wilson in 1916 if they lived near the sites of recent shark attacks. By the same token, voters seem to punish politicians for floods and droughts, but instead of seeking candidates who plan to spend more time or money preparing for such calamities, they simply unseat the incumbent. Time spans are short in attention. A party's economic management is assessed on the basis of only the very recent past. Opinions can fluctuate wildly, depending on how questions are asked. Before the Gulf war of 1991, almost two-thirds of Americans said they were willing to "use military force", but less than thirty percent wanted to "go to war".

The academics know that democratic politics are followed by a few. In Germany half of voters cannot place "*Die Linke*"– "the Left"– on a scale of left to right. Most do not know the name of their representatives. The evidence is that voters tend to pick a candidate first, then bring their policy views into line with their choice. Level of education makes no difference. Thus in their theory of representative democracy James Madison and Edmund Burke alike proposed the trustee model.

It might have been different. The original referendum Bill proposed a "Yes/No" question. Complaints to the Electoral Commission argued this was loaded. "Yes" looks more positive so the question was changed to "Leave" versus "Remain". The number-crunchers said that was a four percent advantage to out. The Prime Minister rejected an attempt by the Lib Dems and Labour to let sixteen- and seventeen-year-olds vote. The reason was purely for party as it would hurt the Conservatives in future elections. Six hundred and fifty thousand votes were lost from that age group. The excluded young are out in Parliament Square in big numbers.

The Vote Leave campaign had written an application filled with gaps. It was rewritten by campaigners late into the night, the final document delivered to the Electoral Commission at 11.40 PM., twenty minutes before the deadline. Had they failed to be the designated official Leave campaign, the debates would all have been led by UKIP. In the event nearly three million votes were cast by women and men who had not voted in an election for decades. The pollsters never got to them.

And yet. It was a choice between status quo and ending an era. But that is as far as it goes. It is the end of something but nothing is clear about what is to come. The population is going to enjoy longevity as never known before but there is small appetite for paid work beyond thirty or so years. A life of thirty years' work and thirty years' non-work is arithmetically impossible for all. It might be possible were Britain a Norway with a small population and a sovereign wealth fund. But it is not. The government taxes, spends and borrows as it goes. In any case chronic ill-health, with depression in the lead, prevents work for a longer span. No referendum can create children to make the gap. An outside body estimates the immigration requirement at one hundred and sixty thousand a year. That is the difference between the vote-casters and government across the river in the ministries that run up Whitehall as far as the eye can see. They look at numbers that are real. The rest of us do not have to worry.

* * * *

Over a table for tea, the hedge funder talks about passporting and double passporting. He is no doubt informed on the facts of his work. Its description is lost on us. "I looked at the facts" says the young Londoner outside Horse Guards Parade. The whole of Whitehall is closed to traffic and the atmosphere is bubbly. The looker-at-facts is twenty-five, a tech entrepreneur and employer of thirty young staff. And, of course, she is an immigrant, here for a few years from Canada. Her facts are simple. Half the new tech sector is funded by foreigners. Berlin, she also says, is chomping for London's tech talent. If she has looked at the facts they are the ones that affect her. In truth there is hardly a voter who could name three things the Commission has done in the last five years. I certainly could not: some run-ins with the Tech Giants over privacy issues and unbundling and that's about it.

Nine-tenths of the thirty thousand in protest are below the age of thirty. "It was a huge emotional hit," says the twenty-year-old language student. "I'm going to Berlin next week. I don't know what I'm going to say to my friends. I'm ashamed to be British." A young Asian on the former Mayor: "I quite liked him as Mayor. I can't believe he just dumped us." This is so far from a first image on television on June 24th. A woman of maturity was in tears. She has, she says, her England back. There is all the difference between those who speak of England and those of Britain.

A younger couple at the tea table, dressed in black, are disappointed the march has not been more earnest. But seriousness need not be earnestness. One group of marchers waves baguettes and carries a banner "Fromage not Farage". A loudspeaker outside the gates to Downing Street plays Schiller's "Ode to Joy". "Shame on you!" runs the chant. Most of the posters are hand-made and there is many a pun on "you" and "EU". "I will always love EU". "EU were always on my mind". These are, it has to be said, the most likely winners in the lottery of life.

But then they are Londoners. The smart tech American knows a lot about city tax takes. She knows how much of its tax dollars Boston and San Francisco gets to keep. "Who do those northern w***ers think pays for them?" I have never heard language of division like this before. But it is the paradox. London pays a quarter of Income Tax, more than north-east, north-west, Humberside and Yorkshire combined. It is the same with tax and business rates. A third of stamp duty is paid within a radius of twenty miles. The north voted against London perhaps for just that reason. There may be trouble ahead but this protest is reassuring. It is so very sunny and British, serious but playful. The devotion to Parliament is affecting. It is an irony since the decision on the referendum never even went, or so it is said, to Cabinet. Peter Hennessy is an acute expert on the inner workings of government. He has this week fallen back on a central plank of national self-belief. "We pride ourselves" he has said, "on being a back-of-the-envelope people."

July 2016: Whitehall, London

Arnold Potts

The best of travel is the serendipity of surprise. The south-western corner of Australia is the smallest blip on the map of the giant mass of the country. It turns out to be a region of daffodils and violets in bloom. At the port of Albany, the "Al" pronounced as in "Alcatraz", the high summer peaks at a low twenty-four degrees. The town of Denmark flocks with parrot, ibis and kookaburra but in September a wood-burning stove has been needed to take the edge off the night chill. The latitude south is the same as Crete and Cyprus in the north; dusk arrives early and briskly. The human population is low so few particulates enter the atmosphere. The last hours of sun, from late afternoon onward, give the sky an intensity of compelling blueness.

Kojonup is on the main highway back to the metropolis of Perth. A man of Kent was once here. Wineries have been set up by the dozen, one on the Kent River. A Tenterden turns out to be a scatter of a few houses and a Cranbook is a couple of miles away. Kojonup was a settlement for cutting down sandalwood and hunting kangaroos. Wool followed. In 1906 the shire had ten and a half thousand sheep. By 1989 they were more than a million. The town sits in a low basin of land fed by fresh water. A military barracks dates back to 1837. The rough building is now the Kojonup Pioneer Museum. In 1900 its population was thirty-two men and thirty-five women. Today the town is a ten-minute walk from one side to the other. Our stroll in the sun comes across a small statue of Brigadier Arnold Potts.

Albany, the end point of the highway, was the port of departure for troops by the thousand on their journey to Gallipoli. It is Australia's most famous name from the First World War. Potts held command at Australia's most significant campaign in the next war. The war in the Pacific has names from the Second World War that are not well-known in Britain. The Battle of the Coral Sea can be seen as an afternoon film that turns up on the minor television channels. Kokoda is a name in Australia that has the resonance of Dunkirk or El Alamein for Britain. A campaign historian, John Laffin, ranks it in toughness alongside Stalingrad and Burma. In strategic importance for the Second World War it stands with the battle of Kursk and the Normandy landings. Australia suffered dozens of air bombings at the hands of the air-force of Japan. But it was Kokoda that forestalled the land invasion.

The naval battles of Coral Sea and Midway in May – June 1942 had prevented a sea borne assault on Port Moresby, the capital of New Guinea. The Japanese High Command determined on an overland assault on Moresby via the Kokoda Track. The Supreme Allied Commander in the South West Pacific, General Douglas MacArthur, knew that the little-known Kokoda Airfield was a threat. Its seizure by Japan would place Port Moresby under direct threat. Major General Basil Morris, the local commander in New Guinea, was ordered to prevent Japanese access across the Track by defending the Kokoda area, roughly half way between Port Moresby and the northern coastal village of Buna. His troops who were rushed forward were poorly equipped and trained. The Japanese soldiers who opposed them had deep experience of jungle fighting.

The islands to the north, New Britain and New Ireland, fell quickly. The landing of two thousand Japanese sixty-five miles from the capital took place on July 21st 1942. The division between Britain and its far-off once-colony was both deep and bitter. Troops from Australia had been dispersed across the Middle East, North Africa and Malaya. The defence in Papua New Guinea comprised under-strength regulars and a few hundred militiamen with an average age of eighteen. The Japanese at their landing points of Buna and Gona captured prisoners from a mixture of plantations, hospitals and mission stations. A small number escaped but most were killed by the invaders. At an Anglican mission, two ministers, two women, two workers, an army officer and, last of all, a six-year-old boy were, one by one, beheaded. The goal, the airfield at Kokoda, was the only point for the defenders to receive supplies from Port Moresby forty-five miles away.

The location of battle was extreme. The northern coast is flat and swampy with rain forest that the sun never penetrates. The Owen Stanley Mountains rise to thirteen thousand feet and are a labyrinth of spurs, ridges, valleys and circling rivers. Tracks were few, steep and muddy in the perpetual wet. New paths had to be hacked out with machete in a dense environment of leeches and malaria-carrying mosquitoes. Japanese snipers tied themselves high up in trees and waited for sight of an officer. Fighting, when it occurred, was one-on-one on terrain the width of a jungle pathway.

The force defending Kokoda cheered at the sight of approaching aircraft with reinforcements. But the planes received false information from headquarters in Melbourne two thousand miles away that Kokoda had fallen. They climbed steeply and disappeared. Equal confusion marked the first battle on the ground, eighty defenders against five hundred. With the commander fatally wounded his replacement, Major Watson, retreated to the village of Deniki. In the jungle another force was engaged in a rear-guard action under atrocious conditions. Soldiers were victim to malaria and dysentery, boots rotted and weapons rusted in the relentless rain. They were without shelter, ground-sheets or blankets for the cold nights. Supplies and food, biscuits and canned meat, were often lost in the air-drops over the jungle.

At Isurava a few hundred men under Lieutenant-Colonel Ralph Honner halted to face four thousand Japanese. Ambushes and raids went on for two weeks until a full-scale offensive by the invaders on 25th August. By that time soldiers from the regular army had arrived. Wave after wave of infantry followed shelling, mortar and continuous machine gun fire. The Australians held Isurava for four days. Brigadier Potts judged that the Japanese advantage in gaining high points threatened the trail, the only route of supplies from the south. After a bloody bayonet charge Potts opted for a slow but deliberate withdrawal.

The role of Potts had been crucial. He devised and implemented the first specific jungle training for Australian troops. Two militia battalions defeated at Kokoda were dug in at Isurava and Alola. These were to join with three battalions under Potts' command. Potts led a fighting withdrawal from Isurava as far as Nauro before being relieved of command. He had discovered a dire shortage of rations. For four days the Australians held off the Japanese who had superiority in numbers and supplies. The Japanese held elevated positions on either side of the main trail and were able to hit the Australians with mortars and machine guns. Threatened with encirclement, Potts withdrew in stages, mounting small delaying actions wherever possible. On 3rd September Potts had received orders from his superior in Port Morseby to hold Myola and gather for an offensive. However, he considered the dry lake bed, surrounded by heights, as untenable. The following day, he signalled: "Country unsuitable for defended localities. Regret necessity abandon Myola. No reserves for counter-attack."

Potts destroyed all supplies at Myola and moved south to the next defensible location, Brigade Hill. He aimed at holding each position for maximum time and at maximum cost to the enemy, before withdrawing. In his assessment he considered that each mile back towards Port Moresby made the Japanese supply and communication line longer and more fragile. The conditions were brutal in the extreme. No wounded could be left. Long after the war Potts said: "We had to sit in the jungle listening to the screams of comrades tortured by the Japanese in an attempt to provoke an attack."

The first stage in halting the Japanese took place two hundred miles to the east, at Milne Bay on the coast. A thousand elite marine troops from naval barges were killed in intense fighting. With their supply lines cut, the Japanese began to retreat. The pursuit by the Australians was arduous, the terrain so bad to impede progress to a mile a day. An ascent of a thousand feet would be followed by a drop of six hundred. Engineers cut steps into the ridges, their record three thousand, four hundred. Every mid-day the rain fell and turned the track to mud. The retreating Japanese resorted to cannibalism of beheaded captives or their own. But on 3rd November the Australians re-entered Kokoda. At a battalion roll call, from an original force of eight hundred, seven officers and twenty-five men were present.

Eventually the retreating troops under Potts joined the main Australian force at Jawarere. At this point the commander of New Guinea Force, Lieutenant General Sydney Rowell, decided to recall Potts to Port Moresby. He was told "the men had shown that something was lacking" and that their leaders were to blame. Potts furiously rejected any blame being attached to his battalion commanders. The verdict after the event supported Potts and the success of his command against the odds.

The retaking of Kokoda found the Japanese survivors riddled with dysentery and starving, despite the recourse to cannibalism. The official war history concluded that Potts' superiors "did not at that time understand so well the circumstances in which Potts found himself and the way he had acquitted himself, genuinely misjudged him". Others were blunter. "It is staggering to contemplate that an Australian brigade commander could be thrust into a campaign with such a damning inadequacy of military intelligence, support and equipment and yet fight a near flawless fighting withdrawal where the military and political stakes were so terribly important and that he could then be relieved from his command as a reward."

Potts' war continued in Bougainville until Emperor Hirohito's declaration of his nation's surrender. Mentioned in despatches twice, he returned home to farm and died on January 1st 1968 at Kojonup, aged seventy-one. The inauguration of the memorial was accompanied by a speech. The appalling physical conditions of Kokoda were recalled as was the nature of the one-on-one fighting with bayonet, boot and grenade. On that day in the open air of Kojonup Potts' decision was vindicated. "The withdrawal was a delaying tactic he had to employ; and he did it well", ran the speech. "He had to concentrate his force, hold as long as possible, make minor counter-attacks and not get overrun. He had to destroy, delay and then set up and do it all over again. In retrospect he achieved the impossible. He stopped a strong, confident and ruthless enemy through personal courage, example and skill. His Brigade's performance along with Maroubra Force was one of the most hard-fought and critical triumphs in Australian military history, and as its commander he deserves the nation's respect and gratitude."

* * * *

My presence on a balmy midday in an Australian Spring in the same place as that speech is accidental, a whim of a stop on a journey. But it has had a cause. Evanses are thick on the ground in Ceredigion and one of them has been in Perth for the last six years. "Newcomers should do their bit for local industry" says Evans-in-Perth as he opens another bottle of wine from the Margaret River region of Western Australia. A stay in a home has many an advantage over hotel or hostel. The choice of food and drink is good. A fridge can be raided at three in the morning by a visitor whose sleep patterns are all over the place. Friends are met. "Did you do National Service?" asks a younger Australian. Either his dates are hazy or my appearance of seniority is greater than I thought.

The answer is the opposite. I was not even there for the battles of the 1960s, although those a little older were in Grosvenor Square. Australians fought in Vietnam and divided the country bitterly. Labour in Britain withstood the greatest pressure to be involved. But in my family the last son among the branch that had emigrated to Canada had died in his aircraft in the Pacific War. From the generation before a great-uncle had emigrated to Australia, not for economic betterment but for health. The climate would be kinder to lungs ruined by gas in the trenches. And now it is a world without conscription with wars fought by the professionals. I have once been near a bomb, once seen a beer bottle broken over a head, and that is it. To see the memorial to Arnold Potts, to remember the boy-men at Kokoda is reminder. A life of now, in the run of things, is pretty much a lucky spin in the roulette wheel of history.

September 2016: Kojonup

Clarice Beckett

The low-ceilinged basement floor of the Art Gallery of South Australia is the end of a quest that began in the National Library of Wales. The gallery on the floor above is the mix common in Britain. Classical architecture of the nineteenth century is melded with open and light-filled additions of the twenty-first century. The below-ground area houses its library, a place of scholarly quiet with just one other visitor besides myself. The librarian has had ready the results of my request. I have come in search of a painter, Clarice Beckett.

One of the items on the table is a catalogue titled *Misty Moderns: Australian Tonalists 1915–1950*. It is the catalogue for an exhibition and tour that took place in Adelaide, and was then taken to Canberra, in February to April 2009. It comprised eighty-two paintings by eighteen artists who belonged to a school that was distinctively Australian. General knowledge of the country's art tends to be dominated by the modernist who came afterwards. Peter Lord in his memoir recounts that Sydney Nolan spent the last decade or so of his life near Presteigne.

Andrew Sayers, a former Director of the National Portrait Gallery of Australia, is author of the volume *Australian Art*. It is part of a series from Oxford University Press and thus available in Aberystwyth. Sayers starts his account of tonalism with the artist Max Meldrum returning home from France. Meldrum arrives armed with a theory of art that is based on principles of science. These he formulates in a book *The Invariable Truths of Depictive Art*.

Sayers, writing from a critical point in time of 2001, is not enthusiastic. The school "produced for the most part gloomy and dull paintings – oppressive portraits in gravy-coloured interiors". But Sayers ends his chapter intriguingly with mention of an artist who is unillustrated. One pupil of Max Meldrum was "to transform the style into a strongly personal idiom, a subtly nuanced ensemble of greys and pinks – almost Whistlerian – and in similar spirit to Whistler – she embraced modernity. All is harmonious in Beckett's paintings – cars, petrol pumps, road signs, beach towels are at one with the grey mists of the morning and the sunset-flushed clouds."

There is another connection of Whistler to the art of Australia. Tom Roberts, the Australian impressionist, met him on a visit to London. But that is the end of the chapter. Sayers moves on to the First World War. Sixty thousand Australians who travelled the highway to Albany never returned. The art in the book moves to a wholly different idiom. George Lambert depicts a troop landing at Gallipoli and Frank Lynch is at the Western Front in France.

As for Clarice Beckett, she is in the Aberystwyth library database as subject of a single monograph. Neither the study, Meldrum's book nor the catalogue *Misty Moderns* are in the Aberystwyth holdings. All three are on the table before me.

Max Meldrum, who lived 1875-1955, had a personality which was a detonator in the quiet world of art of the time in New South Wales. He turned theory into action by opening his own art school. The method he advocated was radical in its novelty. Meldrum's students did not draw, except with the brush. "As if painted with cotton wool rather than a brush", declared a critic. The focus was to "consider with extraordinary care, not only the individual aspects, say, of a jam pot, a bottle and a bit of soap, but also to make an exhaustive and analytical inquiry into their tonal and space relations to one another."

An opponent, Baldwin Spencer, thought Meldrum a "conceited little megalomaniac". A large group exhibition at the Athenaeum

Gallery in Melbourne in 1919 was bitterly received and divided the arts community. The critics abhorred the immediacy of the brushwork and the modesty of subject matter. The subtlety of appearance challenged all the nostrums of an established, nationally-based painting tradition that had emerged, based on high craftsmanship and visual impact.

The critical view from the exhibition ninety years later was more nuanced. "Our tonalism is a conundrum", its curator, Tracey Lock, wrote. "It is progressive on one hand and conservative on the other. Its unassuming, gentle atmospheric aesthetic at times verges on modernist formalism, yet its aim of exact illusions of nature was conservative in intent. Its basis in theoretical concepts was modern, whereas its iconography was conventional." Her conclusion summed up its status. "It has become the most misunderstood and most underestimated movement in Australian art." The state gallery in Sydney, one of significance, groups its paintings around schools and styles of modernism. Tonalism, the one style where Australia did not mirror the art of Europe, goes unmentioned.

Max Meldrum's theory rejected the notion that the eye of the artist should predominate. He looked back to Kant and his *Science of Appearances* for philosophical validation. Tonalism offended the popular preference for paintings of narrative, landscape and a brightness of light. Critically it went against the modern, preferring an indebtedness to Velasquez and Rembrandt with their darkness of tone. To the art critics of the day Meldrum was master "of a cult which muffles everything in a pall of opaque density". The doctrine preached no under-drawing in favour of the painter making rapid and direct recording of tonal impressions. Areas of light and dark are intended as an exact illusion of nature. The result is meditative and low in drama. The difference between the nature of Meldrum's art and the polemical force of his personality could not be more marked.

* * * *

Clarice Beckett was born in 1887 into the middle-class of Victoria. After boarding school in Ballarat she attended grammar school in Melbourne. From 1914 she was at Melbourne's National Gallery School, for three years, where the renowned artist Frederick McCubbin taught. She went on to study under Max Meldrum. Meldrum had declared: "There would never be a great woman artist and there never had been. Woman had not the capacity to be alone."

Beckett had limited opportunity to be alone. In 1919 her parents moved to the Melbourne suburb of Beaumaris. In their old age she assumed control of the family household. These duties set the timetable for the rest of her life. She could go out at dawn and dusk to paint, as she did every day, with a painting trolley and an easel on wheels. The rest of the day was spent on care and household duties. After being out in a storm in July 1935 she contracted pneumonia and died four days later at the age of forty-eight. She had survived her mother by a year and her father died the following year.

Her paintings were exhibited every year from 1923-1934, but they did not sell in large quantities. The critics were unenthusiastic. *The Age* in September 1924 did not like her interest in fogs, even if the colours were pink, blue, green and grey. "Miss Beckett" he wrote, "is probably feeling her way through the fogs and no doubt she will at least rise above the dreariness which characterises her paintings at present." A critical reassessment took decades. In 1971 the National Gallery of Australia bought a group of her paintings. Her sister led a new enthusiast to a shed open to the elements. "There lay one of the most horrendous sights imaginable, rows and rows of rotting canvases." Works from the years from 1918-1933 had been stored in the shed. Of the two thousand paintings two-thirds had been destroyed, eaten by animal or insect or lost in a fire in 1945. In Clarice Beckett's lifetime not a painting was bought by a state or regional gallery. Now some of those which survived are on display in universities and galleries in four states of Australia.

The legacy of Clarice Beckett is a remarkable one, an example of the pupil who went on to outshine the master. She had a greater gift for the manipulation of form than Meldrum. Her subjects are the small exteriors of urban Victoria, suburbs, beaches, a pond, boat sheds and bathing boxes, a cart that passes a line of telegraph poles by dawn. The locations are Beaumaris and Anglesey, San Remo and Menton, all a stone's throw from her home. Much of the work was unsigned but they carry the distinct signature of style. The trees reveal that they could only be in Australia.

There are no edges in the work. The people on a beach are indistinct. Even where she features manufactured objects like the cars of the era or telegraph poles, they have a haziness of edge where they meet their surroundings. Without the sharpness of line for the eye to seize on, they reveal their mystery slowly; a focal point from a five-metre distance suits them well. The hierarchy of value in the Meldrum schema was first tone, then proportion, and lastly colour. Clarice Beckett's colouring is far from the gravy that made critics despair. Primary colours are hardly used and when they are it is done sparingly. The palest of yellow is used for *Yellow Leaves, Alexandra Avenue*. A small parallelogram of blue makes the roof of a beach hut in *Sandringham Beach*. The water under *Prince's Bridge* captures again a pale yellow in reflection of the sky that hardly features in the composition.

The reproductions in the Adelaide library basement are a few feet distant from the real thing. On the floor above a wall of the Gallery has the best of the work. *Passing Trams* was painted in 1931 and only bought in 2001. The gallery in its last hour of opening is quiet and it is possible to carry out an experiment. The picture is available in digital form. At a certain distance from the canvas my eye can flick between two images of the same size. The electronic one on the netbook and the chemical one twenty feet away have the same subject matter. Two city trams nudge past one another in a foggy light. But the images are far apart in quality. The colouring in the digital image does not have the depth or the register of the eighty-five-year-old canvas. The mechanical lens flattens. It favours lines and Clarice Beckett does no lines. Even if it is measurable in only millimetres the painting comes in three dimensions with the weight of pigment applied upon pigment.

The best of travel is discovery by serendipity. It is a long thread and a long journey from a sentence in a book on Bronglais Hill. I am glad to be here. *Passing Trams* is a wonder; its reality has outdone expectation.

September 2016: Adelaide

Our Water Closet Has Been Stopt

Gordon is a residential area nine miles north of Sydney Harbour Bridge. A series of rolling slopes divides the two. By day the train from Berowra, a forest and lake area with protected status, goes straight to the heart of the city. There the towers soar. The greenery and the walks along the waterfront are extensive. Newly married couples from Asia unpack rented bridal wear for photographs against the famous landmarks. A film crew on this day has a drone in the sky capturing aerial footage of the spectacle of nature and architecture in juxtaposition. As usual a film set, even without actors, has two dozen crew, most of them not even watching their drone and camera. Returning on the train from George Street, just before the rush hour, I have the writer Andrew Hassam from Wales for company in the form of his book *Sailing to Australia*.

The origin of *Sailing to Australia* was one of pure happenstance. In September 1987 Hassam was renovating, or rather virtually rebuilding, his house from the foundation stones upwards in Capel Dewi in the Teifi Valley. With the radio for company he heard extracts from the diary of Richard Watt being read aloud. Watt had emigrated aboard the Black Ball Line's *Young Australia* in 1864. That chance programme sparked a curiosity that led first to sight of the original document and from there to the publication of two books.

The first is an anthology of extracts from a selection of diaries all written on board ship en route to Australia in the years 1852-1879. The other, *No Privacy for Writing*, was published by Melbourne University Press in 1995. The earlier book, from 1994, looks at the habit of writing shipboard diaries in its different facets with results that are rich in cultural interest.

The diary-writing of emigrants was not intended as private confession. They were made to be visible and intended for public sharing. William Wills in 1841 writes of himself in the third person, although he declares his aim to be "only for the purpose of amusing himself, and not with the idea that others will derive any gratification from the perusal thereof should it at any period fall into their hands." But then Wills somewhat weakens his case that it is for a private activity by addressing his title page "to his friend Mr John Brownlow".

Edward Towle strikes a similar note in his diary entry for 23rd September 1866. "I am ashamed to send such a specimen to my friends to read, but I have written this journal more for the sake of occupying my mind than with the anticipation that it will afford any gratification or amusement to my friends." But then his account for declared private motives is bereft of all mention of anxiety or fear that were a part of the experience of weeks of sea voyage. The admission of authorship for others is made explicitly by William Hamilton. "The above journal I have written for the amusement and gratification of my father and sisters and now finish it on a very wet and dull day this 17th November 1837."

The diaries rarely dwell on the motives for emigration. It has been a decision of such irreversible consequence that there is no point to its contemplation. Henry Whittington reminds his brother in a letter of 21st June 1852: "Remember that your voyage is for your own benefit, taken voluntarily by you. To lament this, is to lament your own act, and to lament what cannot be undone." Whittington also has firm advice to give to his brother on the rules of a diary. "Your diary must be kept with rigid, puritanic pertinacity. Write in it every day: even, as Cobbett says, though you note but the wind's quarter."

This private injunction had been systematised by W H G

Kingston. Kingston was a chief propagandist for emigration in the 1850s and author of the *Emigrant Voyager's Manual*. He gives suggestions to his reader-travellers as to how they should pass their weeks on the sea. These take in the making of sheep nets out of coconut fibre and carving salt cellars from meat bones. But his manual also has a section on the importance of keeping a diary. "Resolve that nothing shall hinder you from this practice, and depend on it you will often find it assist you in keeping to good resolutions and in avoiding bad habits." The spirit of Samuel Smiles runs through Kingston's *Manual*. Constancy matters. "The journal of the voyage should be written up every day. If the weather is very bad, and you cannot have the ink-bottle out, write it up in pencil."

Kingston is clearly in fear of the danger of developing bad habits. "Make a point of noting down the observations of the Chaplain or religious instructor. Note what trades you learn, and how to occupy yourself. Observe what fishes you see, and describe them. Learn all about them and their habits from the books you have on board." This spirit of improvement runs through to a contention that diaries have at least the virtue of the imparting of knowledge. "To describe particularly a voyage", writes S T Haslett in 1842, "which has been so often described may be superfluous but some things acquainted therewith may be of use and interest." Frances Taylor makes a similar claim to utility in the preface to his diary of 1850. "Should the few lines here penned afford any information which may in any way prove useful to any intending Emigrant or interest any old acquaintance or intimate relative the writer's purpose is fully answered."

This start-point favoured information and utility over the recording of emotional states. The diaries cover varied points of practicality. Thomas Severn advises in his entry of 23rd October 1852 that "a saucepan and frying pan will be found very useful." Conversely he advises against the bringing of cheese. "Mr Tullidge brought a great quantity and it is nearly all spoilt." Benjamin Key on 1st October 1838 gives advice on the selection of cabins. "If any of our friends come out should recommend them to be very particular where their cabins are situated and take care it is not next door to a water closet as our water closet has been stopt and the cabins near to it have a very unpleasant smell." A generation later the voyage has shrunk to six weeks and the conditions are much improved. Thomas Coy has an unusual suggestion on dress. "An indiarubber collar", he writes on 20th February 1885, "will last you a whole voyage and save a lot of time and expense."

This pivoting of diary-writing towards a public readership was of its times. The regional newspapers of Britain were keen to print letters from their former local residents now far off in the colonies. On occasion whole diaries were up for printing. *The Times* published a diary from the first voyage of the SS *Great Britain* to Australia in 1852. A diary by the anonymous "N C" was published as a book. He advises "people never should go to sea without one of those small portable shower-baths, they shew at the Polytechnic, they cost but a few shillings."

The improving tone is one end of the spectrum of record. The other is an honesty of reaction to the journeyers' experiences. Elizabeth Ankatell begins to write nineteen days into her journey on 19th December 1865. "Felt very dreary & lonely & unhappy, could do nothing but cry & wish I had not ventured, everything seemed so confused comfortless and wretched." Solomon Joseph confesses on 28th February 1866: "Everything has been so unsettled that I could not quiet my mind to do anything." Observations of food are common. Isabella Clarke, 10th March 1868: "Oh, if you just tasted what horrible tea we get!" Thomas Trotter in 1836: "Prov gruel twice salt beef & pot." Dullness is relieved by the sightings of fauna. Grace Tindall in November 1856: "Cape hens, cape pigeons, Albatross black and white & Petterilas flying about. A whale in sight on the 30th."

The travellers belonged to the generation which had inherited the Romantic legacy. The efforts made to fit the sights of Australia into a preformed aesthetic schema are considerable and consistent. J Kidd Walpole on 29th October 1837 looks to the coast of his prospective home and sees it "presented all tints, from the faintest hue to the richest purple – in short, all imaginable, or possible varieties, of the spectral hint." Earlier in his journey Felton Matthew, later to become Surveyor-General of New Zealand, passed Madeira. He cast what was passing before his eyes in explicit aesthetic terms: "that rich azure or almost purple, which we see in some of Claud's pictures."

The sighting of land after such an immense distance was cause for thrill. The route often went via Rio de Janeiro to travel with the Trade Winds. "A babel of exclamations was kept up as every new object came into view", writes Alfred Joyce in 1843 on the approach to Port Philip in Australia. "There's a cow, look at it!" is a call recorded by Josiah Hughes in 1863. Closer up to land it yielded disappointment. "On getting closer nearer land I must confess that I was more disappointed by its monotonous outline, regularity of shape in the hills and especially the unvarying colour of the vegetation, than I could well have expected to be" is the view of Richard Watt on 9th August 1864. "N. C." wrote 21st January 1849 of Kangaroo Island: "As for Kangaroo Island, it seems a very uninviting place; nothing but cliffs, sand, and scrub."

The urge to see the familiar in the strange is powerful. William Hamilton, a Presbyterian minister, sails up the River Derwent on 4th September 1837 towards Hobart and sees in the view his native Scotland. "The outline is very like that of Argyleshire. The hills were much like those which environ the Gare loch, on the whole it was the impression of every one that the land was exceedingly beautiful and decidedly surpassed the most admired parts of Scotland in point of scenery." As with the writers, so it is with the artists. John Eyre was one of the first and the Museum of the City of Sydney has one of his works on display. Eyre's subject is Sydney Harbour. It shows a tranquil water in which small boats row past schooners at anchor. Windmills dot the hilltop and the Union flag flies. The land is given a suggestive green of England and the trees are made to resemble the firs and deciduous species of home.

The ambience is one of order, tidiness and discipline. It is far from the actual conditions of Britain's fledgling hold on the fringe of the vast territory to which it laid claim. The colony was a place of turbulence and social and political upheaval. Eyre's image of a quiet prosperity resembled the diaries of the newcomers in being principally a message for home. It would take a century after first arrival before artists would begin to catch the light and the flora that were real.

The streets of Gordon have trees in abundance and they have no resemblance to those that Eyre depicted. Their trunks are fatter than any oak and their foliage is grey. The houses are a medley of styles. Handsome mansions are built in the Federation style. Australia federated in 1906. All visitors to every place of strangeness strain to see the familiar in the new. Look not too closely at a smaller house of wood and it could be the Sussex Weald. Lawns and gardens mimic those from the march-lands of Herefordshire or Shropshire. But the grass that looks like the green grass of home is not. It is tough and springy buffalo grass. Walk on it barefoot at the wrong time and a return to the veranda will reveal leeches adhering to calf and ankle. This area of Gordon is separated from neighbouring St Ives by a gulch a hundred foot deep. It is thick with trees and tracks through the undergrowth are few. The presence of fruit bats ensure its conservation status. Entry is not encouraged for the children of the suburb. A wilderness of this kind is guarantee of vigorous snake life.

In the gloaming, I am persuaded to put the book of diaries aside. As with the beaver six months back in Franconia, nature asks for patience in attendance. A fluffy-headed cookaburra comes in to land on the veranda rail. A wallaby emerges in the half-light on the garden lawn. A little infant head is to be seen in mother's pouch. She snuffles around and finds a nice iris bulb on which to chomp. The best of a foreign land is when it surprises. The Harbour Bridge to the South reverberates with the rumble of railway carriages and six lanes of car, van and lorry. Just a half-dozen train stops away an ecology persists that is much as it has been for millennia. The human habitat of sofa, electronics and fitted kitchen could be anywhere. Step away from it for a minute's walk and it is a location of snake and funnel-web spider with the capacity to kill. The sheer safety of Europe is a result of its centuries of taming and cultivation. It takes the jump to a foreign place to see it in its larger context.

September 2016: Sydney

A Small Blip for Big Gig

The young Canadian is friendly and chatty but it puzzles as to quite what she is doing here on a very ordinary front doorstep in a very ordinary London street. She is a visitor to the capital. She is not visiting family or friends. The nearest historical monument, and that is little visited, is a windmill close to the walls of Brixton Prison. The answer to the puzzle of her presence emerges. It is the Power of the Platform. She is a paying guest of a household host. In the line of houses that we can see, she says, seven have space for rent tonight. The Platform is as omnipresent as it is invisible.

This is not the first time. A queue for day tickets on the South Bank a few weeks previously has been moving sluggishly. In part this is because box office technology demands that every buyer submits much personal data. Try to execute a rapid but anonymous cash transaction and box office staff will politely but firmly refuse. The system will not yield a ticket without a personal data record.

The woman in the velvety cardigan, a companion-in-queuing in her sixties, is primed to chat. It is not quite 9:30 in the morning and this is her third engagement of the day. The first has been common. Helping out a pressed working daughter, she has minded the grandchildren on their route to school. The second engagement is less predictable. She has returned home from the school run to cook breakfast for a dentist from Amman. She has, she confides, lost a husband and the visitor from Jordan in her home is company and a companion in conversation. He is, she says, a morning companion of charm and likeability, but also a nice sixty-five pounds addition to a pension. She is well plugged into the Gig Economy.

That sixty-five pounds is nice to have and an addition to the severe change imposed by a premature widowhood. The Gig Economy is a different issue when it is about trying to make a full-time living. It also puts under the microscope definitions that have traditionally marked and made the status of self-employment.

Britain has a context that is ripe for its flourishing. The rise in self-employment is a feature that divides work from that in Europe. One in seven people is working as self-employed, a percentage that is higher in London and the south-east. Half the new jobs since the crash of 2008 have been self-employed. They can be tough. I passed this season a small and kindly crowd who had gathered around a cyclist-deliverer on the pavement. Nearby was a backpack with its kangaroo company logo. He was shaken but uninjured from his accident. Maybe he had a human supervisor to offer sympathy. By the rules of the Gig Economy his small accident is a service failure.

The Platform has no equal in matching supply and demand. The dominant marketplace for arts and crafts turns over £1.7 billion. Legal documents can be processed for a flat fee. The customer numbers for Big Tech have no precedent. For the leaders it is a one followed by eight zeros. The companies have hardly any assets on their balance sheets and they rank among the most highly valued on the planet. "The new firms are fundamentally empowering because they move the role of the individual from provider of labour to individual owner of the means of production." That is a perspective from a professor at the Stern School of Business at New York University. Big Gig is the name and Data Darwinism is the term from its critics. The New Economics Foundation demolishes the happy talk about partnership. These corporations have partners. They are the investors. If bicycle couriers take a rest that exceeds fifteen minutes they are automatically logged off.

The Platform for potters and knitters is a boon to all involved and invites small regulatory or official attention. The tax authorities keep their eye out for any traders who might hit the threshold for value-added tax registration. No independent craftsperson is going to have a wider rattling effect on the economy. Elsewhere Big Gig and the law are not natural friends. The city of Seattle has advised its drivers to unionise. Cities that levy a tourist tax on hotels for their revenue face a hammering. London's quota of rooms and properties to let is forty thousand. The number in Aberystwyth is a more modest sixty-five.

But the city of Berlin has got tough. Renters of more than half an apartment on a short-term basis need a permit. No permit and the fine is a hundred thousand Euros. Room-letting is fine as long as it keeps below the line of half an apartment. The measure is called the "*Zweckentfremdungsverbot*" or "ban on wrongful use". Property managers lodged a complaint on the grounds that it was unconstitutional in curtailing professional freedom. It is in the high-attraction cities where contention most occurs. London, Berlin, New York and San Francisco all combine huge visitor numbers with growing populations and shortage of rental properties for residents.

* * * *

The reports from employment tribunals do not normally make newspaper front pages. But that is what has happened with Employment Tribunals Case Nos 22025550/2015 & Others. Its verdict has been well summarised in the broadsheets. In its entirety it is a forty page legal document comprising one hundred and thirty paragraphs with notes. It is the first such document I have read and its cultural interest is considerable. The linguistic tones within it come in great variety. A dry and wry eloquence pervades and it reads as British through and through. It is hard to imagine a document from the United States of its like.

The case of drivers versus app is just one of several related complaints but not yet taken to law. Scalper-bots hike the price of tickets for a charity event in aid of sick children. The intermediary Platform states it has no connection with the entertainment business. The biggest distributor of news and not-quite-news is supposed to be a place for mates to chat. Revenues from advertising can give a capitalisation of five hundred billion but it is not a media company.

The industry sectors are different but in each case it comes back to Section 230. Section 230 was created at a time that was very different. In 1996 two congressmen, Chris Cox, a Republican from California, and Ron Wyden, a Democrat from Oregon, drafted a law that they considered essential for the nascent Internet to grow and prosper. The clause that they wrote became statute as section 230 of the Communications Decency Act. That was part of the Telecommunications Act signed into law by President Clinton.

Cox and Wyden had feared libel suits against Internet service providers for content posted on websites that they hosted. The key sentence in the clause reads: "No provider or user of an interactive computer service shall be treated as the publisher or speaker of any information provided by another information content provider." The line goes straight from the Clinton signature in 1996 in Washington D.C. to Employment Tribunals Case number 2202250/2015 in London of October 2016.

The defendants take pains to separate the Platform from the activity. The report cites the rumbustious boss. It is in 2nd February 2016 "an everyday transportation option for millions of people". The tribunal report's authors start with numbers. Four hundred cities are covered in sixty-eight countries. Forty thousand drivers are active in Britain but it is a London thing. Thirty thousand are in the capital. The anomalies begin with the place of jurisdiction. These tens of thousands of working people are governed by the contract law of the Netherlands. Thus the contention of the company is that all employment legislation of the drivers' own country does not apply.

In truth the traditional definition of self-employment had principles but a degree of flexibility. One was the contractor's setting of their own price. The report notes in paragraph 36 that in October 2015 drivers were issued with new terms. The terms were not subject to discussion or consultation. In fact, it was the reverse in that acceptance was necessary for continuing eligibility. One aspect of self-employment is the leeway to provide a substitute, but this is forbidden.

The report digs away at the issue as to who is the customer. The passenger is the customer, but the company is definite it is not an agent. Indeed, an invoice is generated from the driver to the passenger but the passenger never receives sight of it. In a language of care the report says: "He or she would no doubt be vexed to receive it having already paid the fare in full and received a receipt." However, paragraph 23 records that in the occasional case of complaints and refunds a company registered in Britain intervenes with no reference to the driver other than to dock his pay appropriately.

The writers scrutinise the process of becoming a driver in paragraph 40. There is a requirement to attend a physical location and to present documents. To the tribunal it resembles an interview while the company terms it "onboarding". But an email says: "Book an interview NOW!" The focus on the company's language continues with advertising that refers to "our drivers" and "our passengers". The dry comment is "those speaking in the company name have frequently expressed themselves in language which appears incompatible with the central case before us."

Statements have been made to public authorities declaring the company to be "providing job opportunities" and "generating tens of thousands of jobs in the UK". The argument is slipping in the gap between the less guarded language of promotion and the grip of the lawyers. After a review of the appropriate case law, the writers warm up for their analysis and conclusions. Looking at the tangled meanings given to simple terms like "customer" and "invoice" and the corporate nonsense-speak of "onboarding" they conclude: "Any organisation resorting in its documentation to fictions, twisted language and even brand-new terminology, merits, we think, a degree of scepticism." Paragraph 90: "The notion that in London is a mosaic of 30,000 small businesses linked by a common "platform" is to our minds faintly ridiculous." The regional general manager speaks about assisting the drivers to "grow" their businesses, but no driver is in a position to do anything of the kind, unless growing his business simply means spending more hours at the wheel. The absurdity of these propositions speaks for itself.

The writers even turn to literature. A key part of the service is that drivers are hovering in fast reaction to a call. They quote a line of verse, "they also serve who only stand and wait", with the footnote that the quotation is from John Milton. "Reflecting on the case, and on the grimly loyal evidence we cannot help being reminded of Queen Gertrude's most celebrated line: 'The lady doth protest too much, methinks.'" The Californian giant's British manager is female. The footnote accurately records the quotation as being from Hamlet Act 3, Scene 2. An employment tribunal which turns to Milton and Shakespeare in its refutation of corporate flim-flam is cheering. It also feels very British. The judgement is immediately sent for appeal. The company's spokesperson in Britain leaves her role soon after.

October 2016: London

A Pint, a Poet and a Portrait

The biographer of Graham Greene spent years of his life following in the footsteps of his subject. The journey took him to climates as extreme and destinations as volatile as Liberia and Haiti. Mine is a small and placid journey by contrast in the footsteps of literary genius. The biggest hazard has been the rebuilding zone that has been continuous at Tottenham Court Station for years. Even there amidst the scaffolding and cable the murals of Edward Paolozzi are beginning to emerge. From the crowded junction of two main thoroughfares it is a matter of a few minutes' walk through the quiet streets of Fitzrovia. The Post Office tower looms. I saw the view once from high inside before public access was closed after an IRA bombing. Graham Greene's indefatigable biographer was called Sherry. My journey has been timed to coincide with a time that is right for beer.

The Fitzroy Tavern is a building of magnificence. Engraved glass panels stretch to its ceiling which is made of faux-Elizabethan strap-work. Squares of tendrils and bunches of grapes are the repeated theme. The chandelier has its bulbs within twelve globes. The upholstered bench around two walls could seat twenty. The staircases are hung with photographs and pictures from the pub's drinkers and their friends of old. Christopher Wood, Roger Fry, Wyndham Lewis, Lady Ottoline Morrell are all remembered. A portrait of a grim-faced, high-collared matron behind a table with lamp and rolling pin has the signature "N H". It is a picture by Nina Hamnett. A plaque in Tenby marks her birthplace.

The figure from art's history who features most is Augustus

John. The Fitzroy Tavern is where artist and poet met. A twenty-minute walk to the south and a result can be seen. Augustus John's portrait of Dylan hangs among the greats of the twentieth century on the first floor of the National Portrait Gallery. Laurie Lee and T S Eliot are hung as fellow poets to left and right.

The artists who painted portraits of Dylan Thomas were his companions in life. Mervyn Levy recalled an occasion when Alfred Janes picked the poet up. Thomas was turned upside down and shaken until loose change fell out of his trouser pockets. Alfred Janes held that artists across media have some things in common. "One kind of artist understands another", he said, "because he understands some of the possibilities and the potential, the problems and the limitations in which he works."

Janes saw the connections between their arts. "Paintings are made of paint, of shapes, of tonality and texture. Poetry is made of words, the written word is seen but is silent; the spoken word is sound and the written word is shape. Shape and sound call out in the reader, the listener, their meaning." Janes was limitless in admiration. "Of these three kinds of magic Dylan was master. Every letter of the alphabet was to him a performance; it began, it developed and it drew to a close; it had pitch, volume and duration; it also had shape; even alone it was full of meaning. Words were sustained pieces, full of form and cadence. The particular music in Dylan's poetry springs directly from his acute sense of the reality of words as 'things' quite apart from their meanings." Thomas has over the years been well wrapped in waffle. The painter has good things to say.

The first portrait that Janes made was of Thomas aged twenty. The young poet stuffed his mouth with jelly babies through which he discoursed on the sprung rhythm of Gerard Manley Hopkins. The picture shows him in a dark jacket and yellow tie. The reality of the sitting was that the cold in the unheated room sent him to bed in a checked overcoat and pork pie hat. Thomas reminisced on the time. "Years ago, when he was a student at the Royal Academy of Arts, I shared rooms (and what rooms) with Alfred Janes, painter, and those ginger bearded days seem full to me now, of his apples carved in oil, his sulphurously glowing lemons, his infernal kippers. Waking up, one saw all around one the Welsh fires burning behind those fanatically diligent, minutely life-cut, fossil-indented interlogical patterns of rind and scale, and felt like fish on a red-hot flowery slab."

Augustus John also left a written record of the friendship between poet and portraitist. The drinking-holes of Fitzrovia were their regular meeting-place. "I was always glad to meet Dylan in the day-time", said John, "but often gladder still to see the last of him at night." The allure of Thomas' company faded: "when his magic had departed, leaving nothing but the interminable reverberations of the alcoholic." John was not as convinced by the work as a whole, not impressed in particular by *Under Milk Wood*. "The whole hotch-potch", he wrote, "is a humourless travesty of popular life and is served up in a bowl of cold cawl in which large gobbets of false sentiment are embedded. Pouah!"

He did add a conclusion of praise. "Dylan was at the core a typical Welsh puritan and nonconformist gone wrong. He was also a genius." He was also a good sitter for an artist. "Provided with a bottle of beer, he sat very patiently, which is more than I can say for several other distinguished people I could name." The picture by John in the National Portrait Gallery is certainly different from the view of Alfred Janes. It is small, thirteen by eighteen inches in size. Its style is at odds with its frame. John's application of paint has been so free as to leave a small snail's trail of pigment. It sticks out three millimetres from the surface of the canvas and is substantial enough to create its own shadow. His background has zigzags of white. The poet is wearing a large, loose-collared pullover of wool. John has created the pattern of the pullover with a hundred spots and oblongs.

The painting's date is 1937-38, which makes Thomas aged twenty-five to twenty-six. There is no trace of a double chin although the Thomas nose is a prescient red. The psychological interest of the picture is in the contrast between the expression and the features; in their softness it could be mistaken for the depiction of a fourteen-year-old boy. But the gaze into the middle distance is that of maturity. As a portrait it differs from a drawing of the same time by Mervyn Levy. Levy has given the lips an upward twist that imparts a knowing look. The shape of the face has none of the elongation effect of the John. The two images side by side are studies in utter contrast.

As it happens a writer has given a description of precision of Dylan Thomas at the time. The poet that Pamela Hansford Johnson knew wore a pork pie hat. He chose it in the belief that it was the right headgear for a poet. "He revealed a large and remarkable head", she wrote, "heavy with hair the dull gold of threepenny bits springing in deep waves from a precise middle parting. His brow was very broad, not very high: his eyes the colour and opacity of caramels when he was solemn, the colour and transparency of sherry when he was lively, were very large and fine, and the lower rims heavily pigmented. His nose was a blob, his thick lips had a chapped appearance." It is a writer's description, at once precise and general. The fineness of eyes suggests little. It is also writing from the past, the description of the hair colour unclear to those who have never known a threepenny bit. That most lovable of coins was withdrawn in 1971 along with the half-crown and the shilling.

Hansford Johnson picks on one feature that to her eye distinguishes the young Dylan. "His chin was small and the disparity between the breadth of the lower and upper parts of his face gave an impression at the same time comic and beautiful." Alfred Janes caught that disparity in the facial dimensions whereas Augustus John did not. The face that he paints has proportions that meet the average. The distance of nose to lower lip is that of lip to chin. The pupils of the eyes form an equilateral triangle with the top of the philtrum.

But Augustus John makes the national collection. John is a reminder of the judgement about Picasso and Matisse. Picasso was the greater artist but Matisse was the greater painter. It is the tussle between formal ingenuity and thematic fidelity. The painting by Augustus John may be the lesser portrait in its accuracy but it is the greater exercise in artistry of pigment applied to canvas. With its snail trails, its zigzags, its spots and dashes it compels. Alexander Pope discerned something similar when he wrote his 'Epistle to a Lady: Of the Characters of Women' in 1735.

> "Pictures like these, dear Madam! to design,
>   Asks no firm hand and no unerring line;
>   Some wand'ring touches, some reflected light,
>   Some flying stroke, alone can hit 'em right:"

December 2016: Fitzrovia, London

Brits Don't Quit

"It's nice to have someone to talk to." A policewoman is guarding a corner of the square of Lincoln's Inn Fields which is sealed off with police tape. It is the Saturday before Christmas Eve and the Friday night event has been nothing more than an incident spurred by alcohol. The site is awaiting more examination; hence the presence of the policewoman on her own.

Lincoln's Inn Fields is certainly quiet. The fine legal brains who occupy its buildings during the week are at all home. The westernmost block of elegant legal brickwork separates the square from Kingsway so the sound of traffic is subdued. The predominant sound is that of birdsong. People are few; three others in the gardens, the police woman and a man with a white van. The back doors of his van are open and he is unloading fish in ice for carriage into a restaurant basement.

This is the second time in a year I have come to Lincoln's Inn Fields. The first occasion was in February to a lecture theatre in the opposite corner of the square from the former home of Sir John Soane. The Shadow Foreign Secretary was addressing a hall packed with mainly young people. It was a role that Hilary Benn was to cease to perform on June 26th but in February, with the Referendum campaigns in their first stage, he was a speaker of force and conviction.

Benn's father, at the time when he was in the cabinet as Energy Secretary, had sat for the constituency next to the one in which I lived. I had seen him more than once on a public platform. He exuded great charm in part because of the contrast with the members of the Socialist Workers Party and Workers Revolutionary Party whom he attracted. Benn-the-elder sat on a desk in his shirtsleeves with his trademark mug of tea. Benn-the-son in this slight observation of comparison appears the figure of greater political gravity.

Benn-the-father campaigned for "out" in the Referendum of 1975. This time a Benn is arguing for the opposite. His talk has a fourfold argument. He asks for a show of hands as to who has any memory of the time before Britain was member of the Union. Mine is one of a tiny number to be raised. For this young audience, movement for travel, study and leisure is part of the oxygen of their lives, which are admittedly ones of privilege.

Benn recalls figures who are now from history. Jacques Delors galvanised the Unions into altering their stance of suspicion. The result is that the Commission and the Court have been transformed into a joint bulwark of support for employee rights. Abandon their protection and the workers of Britain, says Benn, are at the mercy of heartless neo-liberalism. His point has a weakness in that it presupposes that Labour is incapable on its own of setting the rules for its own country.

The second argument is from experience. There are areas where pooled decisions make for wiser politics. From his experience in Cabinet as Environment Secretary climate change is one such area. The label of sovereignty is loose and lazy. Britain is signatory in his counting to fourteen thousand international accords. Each is in itself a diminution of sovereignty but the signing of each at the time was done for reasons of national advantage. The Commission affects rules on procurement but does not make Britain's policies on education, health, treaties or the making of war. The most ignoble motive in public discourse, he says, is that of blaming the outsider. That raises considerable applause.

His last argument is the least convincing. The Union was an outcome of the settlement of the Second World War. That association was made in the posters across London which featured a Winston Churchill identified as the founder of the European union. The lower case "u" is careful but the poster strapline in Churchillian was "Brits don't quit". Repudiation of the Union, says Benn, is an affront to the memories of those who served and who died. This part of his argument carries the least weight. The official estimate is that between two to three thousand voters of the war generation cast a postal vote but were of such an age they did not live to see the outcome.

The arguments put forward by Benn at that early stage were set on a high plateau of state policy and national inter-working. The months that followed were not. Neo-liberalism has ceased to be a word of denotation and is simply an insult bandied wholesale around the cybersphere. Liberalism itself is on the ropes, but it has been there before. The dispersal of power, the rule of law, political parties and competitive markets are its foundations. The benefits of the last are manifest to the hundreds of millions of migrants of Asia. But the achievements of the liberal era, universal education, public works, employment rights, suffrage, health care, have stalled. Liberalism is not the only language of the public arena that has blurred. The Confederation of British Industry protested the description of narrow product specification as "laws". They are on the statute book but a great bulk of the powers to be repatriated are on the level of a customs coding for a Christmas tree bauble.

In times of challenge, minds turn to history for explanation. One trend of thought declares the real gap with Europe to have been the timing of its revolution. Britain decapitated the monarch and had its glorious revolution too early. Across Europe revolution followed the Enlightenment. Jean André Rouquet, a friend of Hogarth, declared the British to be "slaves to the love of liberty they live in a perpetual fear of losing the least branch of it". Rouquet was not cited in the months of 2016 but he was there nonetheless.

Hilary Benn's fellow Labour Member, Dennis McShane, got into print before year's end. His view on the fifty-seven thousand Europeans working for the NHS was that they were required in Britain because of British failure. The Royal Colleges had clamped down on enrolling the right numbers. McShane recalled that scepticism was built into the relationship right from the start. At the Messina Conference in 1956 a line had circulated whose origin was believed to be Sir Anthony Eden: "Gentlemen, you are trying to negotiate something which you will never be able to negotiate. But if negotiated it will not be ratified. And if ratified it will not work."

* * * *

The purpose of my first visit last winter to Lincoln's Inn Fields was to hear a practitioner of politics. The second this new winter is to see the work of an artist of politics. Art does not teach but it makes the images that bind us. John Soane was born in 1753, eleven years before the death of Hogarth in 1764. He was the successful architect of the Bank of England and the Dulwich Gallery. In 1809 he sold Pitzhanger Manor of his own design and moved to number 13, Lincoln's Inn Fields.

One of his regular places of social gathering was the Foundling Hospital in Bloomsbury. Hogarth had painted the portrait of its founder, Captain Thomas Coram, and donated it to the institution. He had persuaded other artists to do likewise. Hogarth was esteemed for his engravings but his pictures were not held in the same critical regard. Soane bought five large volumes of engravings in the 1790s. He was a self-made man and liked the series of *Industry and Idleness*.

Soane acquired the series *A Rake's Progress* in 1800. In 1823 he bought the *Election* series and that same year bought the neighbouring house, number 14, for its adaptation as a gallery. In the dedication in 1832 to the description of his house Soane wrote of his admiration for "that great moral British artist, William Hogarth". It was a theme that followed the first guidebook to the Soane collections. The author was his friend, the antiquarian John Britton. Britton wrote of the two series:

"These moral, satirical and graphic essays are replete with entertainment and instruction. They are subjects for intense study, not for casual inspection; and, like the profound writings of Shakspeare, or the vivacious and pregnant productions of a Sterne, they afford an exhaustless theme for perusal and reflection."

Britton is quite correct in the quality of repleteness. Hogarth's compositions are filled with allusion, metaphor and a surfeit of detail. But then electioneering in his age lived on surfeit. An entry in the *St James Chronicle* in 1761 listed the requirements for just one election breakfast. The meat comprised thirty-one pigeon pies, thirty-four sirloins of beef, six collars of beef diced, ten cold hams, six dozen sliced tongues, ten buttocks of beef and two hundred and forty-four chickens. To wash this down the drink required, apart from five pounds of coffee, comprised twenty dozen bottles of beer, ten more hogsheads of beer, three of wine and two of punch. The table at Hogarth's *An Election Entertainment* has a heap of oyster shells. Their eater has been so overcome that he needs his forehead to be wiped by a comrade.

The setting is an inn. In the foreground a boy is mixing the punch in a large tub. One of the candidates is being embraced by a large voter. His supporter behind is in encouragement but has set alight the wig of the candidate with embers from his pipe. A young girl eyes the ring on the candidate's finger. The other candidate has the attention of two inebriated voters. One has taken his hand and the other blows smoke over him. The election banner declares "LIBERTY and LOYALTY". A bribe is on offer and another voter points to his shoes that could do with replacing. The election agent has a list of one name, headed "Sure Votes", and a list, "Doubtful", with many names.

Missiles fly in through the open window. An effigy is labelled "No Jews", a reference to a bill of 1753 regarding the exemption of a small number of merchants from taking a Christian oath when applying for naturalisation. The threat of the Other looms in Hogarth's Britain. A huge influx of Jews was feared who along with citizenship would take over national institutions. The government repealed the Act six months later.

The painting has a painting within a painting. A portrait of King William III has been slashed. A political metaphor features in "Canvassing for Votes". The scene is a pub, The Royal Oak, and the landlady has for a seat the figurehead of a ship that shows the British lion eating the French fleur-de-lys. War between the countries was a regular backdrop throughout the century. More bribery is taking place. The election agent is buying gifts from a pedlar to give to two ogling women on a balcony. In the background, symbolically, a saw is being hard applied to the sign of another pub, The Crown. A barber and a cobbler are remembering a great triumph of Britain against the continent. Admiral Vernon captured the town of Portobello in 1839 with just six ships. Now the patriotic ship figurehead is being debased by a pub-owner. Britain was always better in the past.

The Polling features an item of procedural wrangling. A soldier has lost both hands in war and a lawyer is arguing that his hook is no substitute for laying on the Bible. The letter of the law strictly applied prescribes that he does not fit the legal requirement for voting. Behind him Hogarth has painted a voter who is clearly lacking mental competence. In the background Britannia is in a coach that has broken down in the mud. The horses that are supposed to pull it are leaping up on two legs. The door carries the Union Flag of England and Scotland.

The last picture, *Chairing the Member*, is filled with similar allusion. The winner of the election is in danger of falling to the ground. An unsighted fiddler leads the procession and has no inkling of the turmoil behind him. A monkey in jacket and tricorn hat sits on the back of a bear. The bear has his snout in a barrel of offal on the back of a donkey. A sow and her litter charge off a bridge in allusion to the Gadarene swine in the Bible. In the top left of his composition Hogarth has painted an open window. The figure is invisible save for a hand that holds a quill pen. Cut-off from the hurly burly of the political life outside it is the secret hand that writes government policy.

Hogarth's half-hidden figure is a metaphor that speaks on. It ran through the year of referendum. The suspicion was of the hands and unknown faces who write the rules in the shadows. It made no difference that a political scientist wrote of the Commission as subservient to the national governments. The missing voice in the debates was that the Union itself had no part. Hogarth's friend, Jean André Rouquet, thought the British relished any chance of confrontation: "Every thing is conducted in England in the spirit of party and to arouse an Englishman there must be a party to oppose." The Commission was the fall guy. But then we still have the policewomen who say it is nice to have someone to talk to.

December 2016: London

Acknowledgements

Julian Ruddock invited me to the symposium on the Anthropocene. John Harrison sent me the invitation to his reading at the Instituto Cervantes. Susanna Tischler and Christopher Inman were my hosts in Burgweinting. Peter Stevenson reminded me that Gerald of Wales had admired the beavers of Cenarth. Stephen Scholefield has been my guide and window into the world of technology for over thirty years.

Yvonne Murphy alerted me to the demonstration for Europe. Glynne Evans and Helen Bonavita loaned the jeep that made the stop at Kojonup. Kate and Chris Clark told me about the Kokoda Trail and were my hosts in Gordon. Tracey Lock, at the Art Gallery of South Australia, was a mine of knowledge on Clarice Beckett and other artists of her country. Jin Whittington, also in Adelaide, more than fulfilled my requests.

The decision a century ago to locate the National Library of Wales in Aberystwyth has been of inestimable value. Helen Palmer and colleagues at the Ceredigion Archive responded enthusiastically and fulsomely to every request for information. Rebecca Ferguson has never failed to advise correctly on questions of syntax, grammar and expression.

Stephen Mellersh, over many years of conversations, has told me many things on many subjects.

In this, my first experience of working with a professional editor, I have had the benefit of Carly Holmes whose application, accuracy and timeliness have been a model.

Bibliography

Art and the Anthropocene

Gaia Vince; *Adventures in the Anthropocene* (London: Vintage, 2014)

Robert McFarlane; *Landmarks* (London: Hamish Hamilton, 2015)

Robert McFarlane "Generation Anthropocene: How humans have altered the planet for ever" (*Guardian*, 1st April 2016)

Egyptian Spring to Winter in One Hundred and Fifty-Seven Steps

Alaa Al-Aswany; *Democracy is the Answer* (London: Gingko Library, 2014)

Alaa Al-Aswany; *The Automobile Club of Egypt* (Edinburgh: Canongate, 2016)

Doctor Dee and the Exemplar Number of All Things Numerable

Benjamin Woolley; *The Queen's Conjuror* (London: Harper Collins, 2001)

Deborah E Harkness; *John Dee's Conversations with Angels* (Cambridge: University Press, 1999)

185

A Liberal Retrospective

Edmund Fawcett; *Liberalism* (Princeton: University Press, 2014)

Nick Clegg; *Politics* (Oxford: Bodley Head, 2016)

We Became Orphans: A Writer in the Yucatan

John Harrison; *1519: A Journey to the End of Time* (Swansea: Parthian Books, 2016)

Alfred W Crosby; *The Columbian Exchange* (Westport, Connecticut: Greenwood Press, 1972)

A Visit to the Cloud

Andrew Blum; *Tubes. Behind the Scenes at the Internet* (London: Viking, 2012)

"Finding a Voice" *The Economist Technology Quarterly* (London, November 2016)

Wherever There is Arbitrariness, There Is Also a Certain Regularity.

Peter Calvocoressi; *Top Secret Ultra* (London: London, 1980)

Tessa Dunlop; *The Bletchley Girls* (London: Hodder and Stoughton 2015)

Sinclair Mackay; *The Secret Life of Bletchley Park* (London: Aurum, 2010)

War: What Is it Good For?

Ian Morris; *Foragers, Farmers and Fossil Fuels* (Princeton: University Press, 2015)

Ian Morris; War: *What Is It Good For?* (New York: Farrar, Strauss and Giroux, 2014)

The Digital Superhighway

Edited Tilly Blyth; *Information Age. Six Networks that Changed Our Age* (London: Scala Arts, 2014)

Christian Rudder; *Dataclysm* (London: Fourth Estate, 2014)

Waiting for a Beaver

Timothy Brook; *Vermeer's Hat* (London: Profile, 2008)

Gerald of Wales; *The Journey Through Wales* (Harmondsworth: Penguin, 1978)

Scottish Wildlife Trust:
https://scottishwildlifetrust.org.uk/news/beavers-back-for-good/

I'll Swap You Two Buggers for a Shit

Geraint Talfan Davies; *At Arm's Length* (Bridgend: Seren, 2008)

Jean Seaton; *Pinkoes and Traitors* (London: Profile, 2015)

John Tusa; *Pain in the Arts* (London: I B Tauris, 2014)

An Elephant in Bremen

Richard J Evans; *The Third Reich in History and Memory* (London: Abacus, 2015)

The Hate Horrifies Me

Svetlana Alexeivitch; *Second-hand Time* (London: Fitzcarraldo, 2016)

Oliver Bullough; *The Last Man in Russia* (London: Allen Lane, 2014)

Who Needs Empathy?

Daniel Susskind and Richard Susskind; *The Future of the Professions* (Oxford: University Press, 2016)

I Long the Arrival of the Ship with the Seeds

Andrea Wulf; *The Brother Gardeners* (London: William Heinemann, 2008)

Caroline Palmer, Penny David and Ros Laidlaw; *Historic Parks and Gardens in Ceredigion* (2004 Welsh Historic Gardens Trust, Esgairdawe)

An Occasional Flash of Silliness

Peter Dickinson; *Lord Berners* (Woodbridge: the Boydell Press, 2008)

David Long; *English Country House Eccentrics* (Brimscombe Port: History Press, 2012)

The Map-makers

Simon Garfield; *On the Map: Why the World looks the Way it Does* (London: Profile, 2012)

Edited Tom Harper; *Drawing the Line* (London: The British Library, 2016)

Kapka Kassabova; *Border* (London: Granta, 2017)

A Citizen's Guide to the European Union

Chris Bickerton; *The European Union: A Citizen's Guide* (London: Pelican, 2016)

They Are Obsessed by Fear

Gabriel Zucman; *The Hidden Wealth of Nations* (Chicago: University Press, 2015)

Nicholas Shaxson; *Treasure Islands* (The Bodley Head: Oxford 2012)

Among the Demonstrators

Dennis McShane; *Brexit. How Britain Left Europe* (London: I B Tauris 2016)

Sonia Purnell; *Just Boris: A Tale of Blond Ambition* (London: Aurum Press, 2012)

Arnold Potts

Philip Knightley; *Australia. The Biography of a Nation* (London: Jonathan Cape, 2000)

Max Hastings; *All Hell Let Loose: The World at War 1939-1945* (London: HarperPress, 2012)

Clarice Beckett

Rosalind Hollinrake; *Clarice Beckett: Politically Incorrect* (Melbourne: Ian Potter Museum of Art, 1999)

Tracey Lock-Weir; *Misty Moderns – Australian Tonalists 1915–1950* (Adelaide: Art Gallery of South Australia, 2008)

Andrew Sayers; *Australian Art* (Oxford: University Press, 2001)

Our Water Closet Has Been Stopt

Andrew Hassam; *Sailing to Australia* (Manchester: University Press, 1994)

A Small Blip for Big Gig

https://www.judiciary.gov.uk/wp-content/uploads/2016/10/aslam-and-farrar-v-uber-reasons-20161028.pdf

A Pint, a Poet and a Portrait

Hilly Janes; *The Three Lives of Dylan Thomas* (London: Robson Press, 2014)

Augustus John; *Finishing Touches* (London: Jonathan Cape, 1964)

Brits Don't Quit

Jenny Uglow; *Hogarth: A Life and a World* (London: Faber and Faber, 1998)

Index of Places

Abersoch 30

Aberystwyth 6, 9, 11, 12, 26, 72, 81, 102, 153, 154, 168

Adelaide 153, 157

Afghanistan 60

Alaska 12, 120

Albany 137, 146, 154

Alexandria, Egypt 15

Algeria 82

Alola 149

Amman 166

Andes 36

Anglesey, New South Wales 157

Anguilla 135

Annam 120

Antarctica 36

Antibes 35

Antioch 59

Apia 83

Appalachians 107

Arctic 47, 48

Arctic Circle 46

Argyll 69

Babylon 57

Ballarat 156

Barry 31

Bath 113

Bayswater 39, 40

Beaumaris, New South Wales 156, 157

Beijing 132

Belarus 69, 87, 89, 93

Belgium 26, 27

Belgravia 35, 36

Berkeley, California 132

Berlin 52, 81, 84, 130, 138, 144, 168

Bern 135

Berowra 159

Bismarck Archipelago 82

Bismarck Sea 82

Blaeneinion 68

Bletchley Park 51, 52, 53, 54, 55, 118, 123

Bloomsbury Square 10

Bloomsbury 180

Bonampak 37

Bonn 29, 54

Boston 43, 145

Bougainville 82, 151

Boulogne 28, 114

Brazil 43, 109, 120

Brecon 109

Bremen 82, 85, 86

Bristol Channel 12

Brixton 75, 166
Bronglais Hill 158
Buchenwald 81
Buckingham Palace 114
Buna 147, 148
Burgweinting 70
Burma 124, 147

Cabo Catoche 39
Cairo 14, 18
Cambridge 1, 22, 23, 81, 126, 127
Cameroon 83
Campeche 39
Canada 31, 42, 68, 122, 144, 152
Canarch Mawr 67
Canberra 153
Cape Verde Islands 42
Capel Dewi 159
Cardiff 109, 118
Caroline Islands 82, 83
Casablanca 121
Castile 44
Cayman Islands 36, 133, 136
Champoton 39
Chamula 38
Chelsea 104, 105, 108
Chernobyl 92
Chiapas 38
Chicago 109, 110, 132
Chiltern Hills 119
China 69, 88, 102, 120, 132
Clarach, River 110
Cleobury Mortimer 51
Cochin China 120
Colombia 120

Columbus River 46
Coral Sea 147
Coriander Avenue 49
Cothi, River 109
Cranbook 146
Crow Creek, South Dakota 60
Cuba 42
Cuernavaca 38
Cyprus 82, 146

DDR, the German Democratic Republic 8, 81
Delaware 107, 137
Deniki 148
Denmark 31, 146
Derwenlas 26
Derwent, River 163
Devon 69, 113
Didcot 113
Dnieper, River 87
Dover 28
Downing Street 49, 50, 73, 95, 145
Dubai 67
Dulwich 180
Dunkirk 147
Dyfi, River 9, 26

Eaton Square 35
Ecuador 120
Edinburgh 77
Edwinsford 109
El Alamein 147
Elan Valley 48
Enewetak Atoll 83
Espirito Santo 41

Essex 107
Eton 126
Exeter 69
Extremadura 37

Faringdon 112, 113, 115, 116
Fez 121
Finchley 74
Finland 47, 69
Fitzrovia 172, 174
Forth, Firth of 115
France 16, 27, 28, 31, 32, 57, 69,
     128, 113, 153, 154
Frankfurt 34

Gallipoli 28, 147, 154
Germany 1, 2, 27, 28, 29, 32, 52,
     55, 69, 81, 82, 83, 84, 85, 86,
     103, 110, 119, 122, 124, 127,
     143
Gogerddan 109, 110
Gona 148
Goodwood 106, 107
Gordon 159, 164
Grand Turk 135
Greece 27, 127
Greenland 3, 8, 120
Gregynog 26
Grindelwald 11
Grosvenor Square 152

Haiti 172
Hamburg 34, 110
Hamina 47
Hampstead 138
Hay-on-Wye 87, 95

Heilongjian 88
Herefordshire 164
High Wycombe 118
Hobart 163
Hollywood 58
Hoover Dam 48
Huddersfield 27
Hughenden 118, 119, 122, 123,
     124
Humberside 145
Hyde Park 137

Iceland 42
Illinois 16, 18
Iowa 46
Iraq 60
Isurava 148, 149

Jaluit Atoll 83
Japan 31, 55, 64, 83, 147, 148,
     149, 150
Jawarere 150
Jersey 135

Kaliningrad 131
Kangaroo Island 163
Kensington 30
Kent River 146
Kenya 82
Kew 104, 109
Kingsway 177
Knapdale Forest 69
Knightsbridge 137
Kojonup 146, 151
Korea 136
Kursk 147

Lagos 101
Lampeter 72
Leon 44
Liberia 172
Lidice 119
Lincoln's Inn Fields 128, 177, 180
Lincolnshire 108
Llanbedrog 30
Llandrindod Wells 109
Llanwrtyd Wells 109
Louvain 21
Lubyanka Square 92
Luleå 46
Luxembourg 132, 133

Machynlleth 10, 68
Madeira 163
Madrid 37
Malaya 124, 147
Malvern Hills 79
Mametz Wood 118
Manchester 27, 136
Margate 140
Marseilles 120
Marshall Islands 82, 83
Maspero Square 15
Massachusetts 43
Medellin 37
Medway, River 12
Melbourne 148, 155, 156
Menton 157
Mesopotamia 57
Messina 180
Mexico City 7
Miami 46, 47

Milne Bay 150
Minsk 93
Mohamed Mahmoud Street 15
Mongolia 69
Monte Cassino 123
Montreal 20
Mortlake 23
Moscow 88, 93
Munich 12
Myola 149

Namibia 85, 86
Nauru 82
Nechells 141
Netherlands, The 68, 170
Nevada 136
New Britain 147
New Ireland 147
New Jersey 142
New York City 57, 64, 137, 167, 168
New Zealand 12, 83, 109, 163
Newport 46, 49
Normandy 147
North Carolina 46
Norway 69, 133, 144
Nuremburg 71
Nutmeg Lane 49

Oran 121
Oregon 46, 49, 169
Owen Stanley Mountains 148
Oxford 27, 105, 106, 113

Paddington 39, 113
Pall Mall 114

Panama 41
Paris 19, 22, 114, 120
Parliament Square 138, 143
Pembrokeshire 39
Pennsylvania 130
Perm 91
Pernambuco 41
Peru 41, 42
Peterborough 142
Philadelphia 106
Philippines, The 35
Piccadilly 137
Pilleth 21
Pitzhanger Manor 180
Plas Dinam 26
Plymouth Bay 43
Pontcanna 40
Port Moresby 147, 148, 149, 150
Port Philip 163
Portobello 182
Portugal 127
Poznan 53
Prague 24, 34
Presteigne 153
Puebla 38, 39

Regensburg 70
Regent's Park 21
Rhosygilwen 39
Rio de Janeiro 41, 63
Rio de la Plata 41
Roanoke Island 42
Romania 15
Rome 57, 59
Rosemary Drive 49

Russia 31, 41, 69, 87, 88, 89, 93, 94, 130, 131, 132

Saigon 120
Saltaire 26, 29
Samoa 82, 83
San Francisco 145, 168
San Remo 157
Sandhurst 126
Santa Barbara 8
Santa Domingo 42
Sarajevo 119
Saudi Arabia 19
Scotland 69, 76, 136, 163, 182
Seattle 168
Severn, River 26, 29
Shipley 27, 29
Shropshire 26, 164
Siberia 91
Singapore 131, 133
Sledmere Hall 114
Snowshill Manor, Cotswolds 113
Soho Square 109
Solomon Islands 82
Somerset 69
South Africa 85
Southampton 113
Spain 31, 36, 37, 38, 41, 127
Spalding 140
St Augustine 42
St Ives 164
St Petersburg 90
Stalingrad 120, 147
Suez Canal 20
Surrey 131
Sussex 107, 131, 164

Swansea 134
Sweden 47, 49, 69, 105
Swindon 113
Switzerland 2, 47, 49, 119, 132
Sydney 155, 159, 164
Syria 82

Tahiti 109
Talerddig 26
Taliesin 10
Tay, River 69
Teifi, River 67, 68, 159
Tenby 172
Tenochtitlan 36
Tenterden 146
Tewkesbury 121
Texas 46
Thames, River 23, 138
Thorndon 107
Tierra del Fuego 43
Tipton 141
Tlaxcala 37
Togo 83
Tokyo 122
Tonkin 120
Torfaen 150

Tottenham Court Road 172
Trujillo 37

Ukraine 87, 89

Vera Cruz 37
Vietnam 120, 135, 152
Vindolanda 2, 59
Virgin Islands 132
Vistula, River 87

Wash, The 29
Westminster 27, 30, 139
White Sea Canal 92
Whitechapel 62, 65, 66
Whitehall 22, 95, 138, 144
Williamsburg 109
Winchester 112
Woburn 106
Worcester 141

Yorkshire 145
Yucatan 36, 37, 38, 42

Zurich 29

Index of People

Achen, Christopher 142
Acton, Lord 32
Aguilar, Francisco de 43
Al-Aswany, Alaa 14
Al-Buhairi, Bishwi 15
Al-Khattab, Umar Ibn 17
Alexandra, Queen 114
Alexeivitch, Svetlana 89
Allen, Jim 78
Ankatell, Elizabeth 162
Applebaum, Anne 87, 88
Ashton, Frederick 116
Astor, Alice 116
Attlee, Clement 28, 32

Baggins, Bilbo 120
Bakr, Abu 17
Balanchine, George 116
Baldwin, Mark 51, 52, 53, 55
Baldwin, Stanley 35, 118
Banks, Joseph 108, 109
Bartels, Larry 142
Bartram, John 106, 107
Beaton, Cecil 116
Beaverbrook, Lord 116
Beckett, Clarice 2, 153, 154, 156, 157, 158
Bedford, Duke of 106

Beerbohm, Max 116
Behr, Winrich 120
Bell, Clive 116
Benn, Anthony Wedgwood 75
Benn, Hilary 27, 28, 177, 178, 179, 180
Berlin, Isaiah 116
Betjeman, John 114
Bevan, Aneurin 32
Beveridge, William 32, 33
Bevin, Ernest 32
Bickerton, Chris 125, 126, 127, 128, 129
Bismarck, Otto von 82
Blaeu, Willem 120
Blair, Tony 32, 102
Blake, William 11
Bleasdale, Alan 78
Bodin, Jean 23
Brahe, Tycho 23
Braudel, Fernand 37
Brecht, Bertolt 131
Brenton, Howard 77
Breuning, Olaf 63
Bridgewater, 8th Earl of 114
Briggs, Asa 72
Britton, John 181
Brown, Gordon 77

Brownlow, John 160
Bullough, Oliver 88, 89
Burgess, Anthony 6, 9
Burke, Edmund 142, 143

Caesar, Julius 57
Cairncross, John 54
Carrington, Lord 28
Casati, Luisa 115
Castelnau, Michel de 23
Caxton, William 98
Cecil, William 22
Champlain, Samuel de 68
Chance, Leonard 124
Churchill, Winston 29, 115, 179
Cicero 68
Clarke, Isabella 162
Clayton, Aileen 54
Clegg, Nick 30
Clifton, Geoffrey 121
Clinton, Bill 169
Cobbett, William 160
Collinson, Peter 106, 107
Connery, Sean 35
Cook, James 108
Copernicus 23
Coram, Thomas 180
Córdoba, Hernandez de 42
Cornwell, David 29
Cortes, Hernan 36, 42, 44
Cox, Chris 169
Coy, Thomas 162
Cranston, Bryan 97
Cromer, Lord 17
Cromwell, Oliver 142
Cruise, Tom 78, 97

Crutzen, Paul 7
Cubitt, Thomas 21
Cuitlahuac 42
Curran, Charles 74
Czikszentmihalyi, Mikhail 102

Dali, Salvador 3, 116
Davies, David 26, 27, 28, 31, 34
Davies, Evan 140
Davies, Lord and Lady 26
Davy, Humphrey 3, 11
Ddu, Bebo 21
De Las Casas, Bartolomé 41
Dee, John 3, 21, 22, 23, 24, 25
Dee, Rowland 21
Delors, Jacques 29, 127, 178
Deniston, Alastair 54
Descartes, René 3, 128
Diaghilev, Serge 115
Diaz, Bernal 38
Donne, John 39
Drake, Francis 42
Dudley, Robert 22
Dzerzhinsky, Felix 92

Easterby, Jony 9
Eden, Anthony 180
Edward VI 21
Eissa, Ibrahim 15
El-Adly, Habib 18
Elgar, Edward 79
Eliot, T S 173
Elizabeth I 21
Euclid 22
Evans, Richard 81, 82

Eyre, John 163, 164

Farage, Nigel 145
Farouk, King 17
Fearnley, Thomas 11
Fellowes, Julian 78
Felton, Matthew 163
Fichte, Johann Gottlieb 3, 128
Fitzgerald, Penelope 79
Fonteyn, Margot 116
Francis, Jane Lloyd 10
Fry, Roger 172
Fuad I, King 17

Garibaldi, Giuseppe 140
Gasset, Ortega de 127
George III 109
Gerald of Wales 67, 68, 70
Gerald, John 11
Gibb, Robin 35
Gladstone, William 32, 33
Goering, Hermann 85
Gorbachev, Mikhail 93, 94
Greene, Graham 38, 172
Grimond, Jo 27

Habermas, Jürgen 128
Hadid, Zaha 96, 98
Hague, William 46
Hamana, Henare 12
Hambrey, Mike 11
Hamilton, William 160, 163
Hamnett, Nina 172
Händel, Friedrich 11
Hannan, Daniel 140
Harcourt, William 33

Hare, David 77
Hariot, Thomas 42
Harrison, John 36, 37, 38, 39, 40, 41
Haslett, S T 161
Hassam, Andrew 159
Hatton, Christopher 22
Healey, Dennis 28
Hegel, Georg Wilhelm Friedrich 127
Heidegger, Martin 73, 98
Hemingway, Ernest 9
Hennessy, Peter 1, 141, 145
Henry VII 22
Henry VIII 22
Herder, Johann Gottfried 128
Herivel, John 52
Herr, Michael 120
Herrera, Antonio de 41
Hertzfeld, Andy 45
Hirohito, Emperor 151
Hogarth, William 1, 128, 139, 179, 180, 181, 182, 183
Holmes, Arthur 6
Honner, Ralph 148
Hopkins, Gerard Manley 173
Huayna Capac 42
Hudson, Kathlyn 124
Hughes, Josiah 63
Humboldt, Alexander von 103

Irving, David 81

James, Edward 116
Janes, Alfred 173, 174, 175
Jenkins, Roy 29

Jersey, Earl of 106
John, Augustus 172, 173, 174, 175, 176
Johnson, Boris 6
Johnson, Pamela Hansford 175
Jones, Indiana 121
Joseph, Solomon 162
Joyce, Alfred 163
Juvenal 68

Kant, Immanuel 155
Kapic, Suada 119
Kaprow, Allan 64
Kasparov, Garry 87
Kekulé, August 10
Kendall, Bridget 89, 90, 91
Kepler, Johannes 23
Key, Benjamin 162
Keynes, John Maynard 32
Kingston, W H G 161
Kinnock, Neil 102
Klüver, Billy 64
Knox, Dilwyn 53
Kray, Ronnie 62
Kuebler-Ross, Elisabeth 40
Kurzweil, Ray 61

Laffin, John 147
Lambert, George 154
Landa, Diego de 42
Langston, Robert 121
Lannister, Tyrion 139
Lasdun, Dennis 21
Le Carré, John 29
Lee, Laurie 173
Leigh, Vivien 115

Lenin, Vladimir 90
Leon, Cieza de 42
Levy, Mervyn 173, 175
Lewis, Wyndham 172
Linnaeus, Carl 105, 106, 108, 109
Lloyd George, David 32, 33
Lock, Tracey 155
Lord, Peter 153
Lorrain, Claud 163
Lowry, Malcolm 38
Ludoc, Saint 67
Lynch, Frank 154

MacArthur, Douglas 147
Macklin, Mark 10, 11
Madison, James 143
Malevich, Kasimir 65, 98
Marx, Karl 58, 61
Mason, Roy 75
Matisse, Henri 176
McCubbin, Frederick 156
McDermid, Val 50
McElvoy, Ann 141
McShane, Dennis 180
Meldrum, Max 153, 154, 155, 156, 157
Memling, Hans 11
Mercator, Gerardus 21
Mercer, David 78
Metternich, Klemens von 35
Michaelangelo 11
Mill, John Stuart 31, 33, 73
Miller, Philip 104, 105, 108
Milton, John 171
Mondrian, Piet 64

Monnet, Jean 127
Montezuma 42
Morrell, Ottoline 172
Morris, Basil 147
Morsi, Mohamed 15, 19
Morton, Timothy 12, 13
Motolinio, Toribio 42
Mubarak, Alaa 18
Mubarak, Gamal 18
Mubarak, Hosni 16, 17

Nasser, Gamal 17
Newton, Isaac 11
Nicholas II 90
Nolan, Sydney 153
Norderland, Miran 119
Nujoma, Sam 86

Offe, Claus 128
Oldman, Gary 78
Olivier, Laurence 115
Orozco, José Clemente 37
Ortelius, Abraham 23
Orwell, George 3, 142
Owen, Alun 78
Paget, Henry Cyril 113
Paik, Nam June 62
Paolozzi, Edward 172
Paracelsus, Theophrastus von
  Hohenheim 103
Parker, Mike 119
Parry, William 109
Peabody, George 135
Petre, 8th Baron 107
Picasso, Pablo 67, 176
Pizarro, Francisco 37

Plato 23, 99
Pope, Alexander 104, 176
Porter, Michael 102
Potter, Dennis 2, 40
Potts, Arnold 146, 147, 149, 150,
  151, 152
Putin, Vladimir 87
Pythagoras 24

Qandil, Hamdi 15
Queensbury, Duchess of 104

Rahma, Dina Abdel 15
Raleigh, Walter 23
Rauschenberg, Robert 64
Reiche, Momoe von 83
Rejewski, Marian 53
Rembrandt 155
Rhodri the Great 21-22
Richmond, Duke of 106
Riley, Jonathon 118
Rivera, Diego 37
Roberts, Tom 154
Rokeby, Lord 114, 115
Roosevelt, Franklin D 31
Rothschild, 2nd Lord 114
Rouquet, Jean André 179, 183
Rowell, Sydney 150
Rozycki, Jerzy 53
Rudolf II 24
Russell, Ken 79

Saad Zaghlould, Saad 17
Sadat, Anwar 17
Sadqi, Isma'il 17
Salina, Fabrizio 140

Sandbrook, Dominic 58
Sassoon, Siegfried 116
Sayers, Andrew 153, 154
Shakespeare, William 5, 11, 40, 171
Scherbius, Arthur 52
Schiller, Friedrich 145
Schmidt, Eric 50
Schneider, Friedrich 134
Schulze-Delitzsch, Franz Hermann 32
Seaton, Jean 72, 73, 74, 76, 78, 79
Sedgley, Peter 64
Severn, Thomas 161
Shaw, George Bernard 17
Shaxson, Nicholas 135, 136, 137
Shenouda III, Pope 20
Sherry, Norman 172
Shore, Peter 74
Sidney, Philip 22
Siegesbeck, Johann Georg 106
Silver, Long John 121
Siqueiros, David Alfaro 37
Sitwell, Edith 113, 116
Smiles, Samuel 161
Snow, C P 22
Soane, John 128, 177, 180, 181
Socrates 65
Solander, Daniel 108, 109
Solzhenitsyn, Alexander 92
Soprano, Tony 87
Spee, Maximilian von 83
Spencer, Baldwin 154
Stalin, Josef 91, 92
Steel, David 27
Stein, Gertrude 116

Steyerl, Hito 66
Stoermer, Eugene 7
Strauss-Kahn, Dominique 57, 60
Stravinsky, Igor 115
Streeck, Wolfgang 128
Sultan, Doaa 15
Susskind, Daniel 95, 96, 97, 98, 99, 100
Susskind, Richard 95, 96, 97, 98, 99, 100
Swann, Michael 76, 77
Swann, Tess 76, 77
Sykes, Tatton 114
Szilard, Leo 10

Talfan Davies, Geraint 80
Taylor, Frances 161
Tebbit, Norman 75
Thatcher, Margaret 29, 73, 74, 75, 77, 78
Thomas, Dylan 1, 173, 174, 175
Thomas, R S 6
Tindall, Grace 162
Topol, Eric 97
Towle, Edward 160
Trismegistus, Hermes 23
Trotha, Lothar von 83
Turing, Alan 54, 55
Tyrwhitt-Wilson, Gerald Hugh 112

Urabi, Ahmed 17

Velasquez, Diego 155
Vermeer, Johannes 68, 120
Vernon, Edward 182

Wade, Charles Paget 113
Walker, William 112
Wallace, William 26, 27, 28, 29, 30, 33, 34
Walpole, J Kidd 163
Walsingham, Francis 22
Walton, William 116
Warren, Julianne Lutz 12
Watt, Richard 159, 163
Waugh, Evelyn 116
Weber, Max 70, 127
Wells, H G 116
Weyl, Herman 25
Whistler, James Abbott McNeill 154
White, Walter 27
Whitelaw, William 28
Whittington, Henry 160
Wiggen, Ulla 64

Wild, Johanna 21
William III 182
Wills, William 160
Wilson, Harold 74
Wilson, James 31
Wilson, Woodrow 142
Wood, Christopher 172
Woolf, Virginia 114
Wulf, Andrea 103, 104, 106, 107, 110, 111
Wyden, Ron 169
Wyn Jones, Richard 140

Yeltsin, Boris 90, 93

Zucman, Gabriel 97, 132, 133, 134, 135, 137
Zygalski, Henryk 53

PARTHIAN *Essays*

Notes from a Swing State
Writing from Wales and America
Zoë Brigley Thompson
ISBN 978-1-912681-29-7
£8.99 ● Paperback

'... startlingly beautiful imagery ...'
– *Planet Magazine*

Between the Boundaries
Adam Somerset
ISBN 978-1-912681-36-5
£8.99 ● Paperback

'... accomplished collection which
engages, inspires and entertains.'
– *Jon Gower*

Driving Home Both Ways
Dylan Moore
ISBN 978-1-912109-99-9
£8.99 ● Paperback

Travel writing from the Creative Wales
Hay Festival International Fellow

Seven Days
Nathan Munday
ISBN 978-1-912109-00-5
£8.99 ● Paperback

'...a beautiful, wise, and moving book.'

– *Niall Griffiths*